W9-AHJ-479

THE WOODEN LEG OF
INSPECTOR ANDERS

The Wooden Leg of Inspector Anders

Marshall Browne

THOMAS DUNNE BOOKS / ST. MARTIN'S MINOTAUR ♊ NEW YORK

THOMAS DUNNE BOOKS
An Imprint of St. Martin's Press

www.minotaurbooks.com

ISBN 0-312-27838-1

First published in Australia by Duffy & Snellgrove

First St. Martin's Minotaur Edition: May 2001

10 9 8 7 6 5 4 3 2 1

THE WOODEN LEG OF
INSPECTOR ANDERS

I

MONDAY

THE EXPRESS FROM ROME pushed its blunt nose into the southern city's central station at one minute past four o'clock. It eased to a halt in the deep shadow of the cavernous, begrimed structure, built as a fascist national project in 1931. Inspector Anders took his suitcase, and quite easily stepped down to the platform. Despite his artificial leg his movements were efficient, with only the slightest dislocation to their rhythm. The disembarking passengers streamed through the barrier gate, and in his unobtrusive way Anders went with them. Casually, he glanced at the faces of those who waited, arrayed in a crescent around the gate. Expectant faces, faces drugged with waiting. He wasn't expecting to be met, but for many years he'd been careful with his expectations.

What a place! It was as cold and echoing as a vast tomb. The distorted announcements coming from the PA system had an eerie otherworldliness, which serrated the nerves. He shivered despite his overcoat. There was no-one to arouse his suspicions. Only the usual steely-eyed police standing in pairs, bored with their assignment, with each other. His eyes found a blaze of colour in the gloom – a stall of sunflowers. He sighed with pleasure at the rich, earthy colours, his old memories of the south, the women of this region! Much was coming back to him. He did not go to the taxi rank, but walked some fifty metres away from the station's main entrance, an aperture of Gargantuan proportions, braced by stone columns rather crudely cut in the Corinthian order. In winter, he recalled that overwhelming blasts of wild weather came in. He stared across the piazza to the cafe that still bore the scars of the bomb which, on the tenth of July, had blown up Investigating Magistrate Fabri and his two bodyguards. As though paying homage, he stood there for several minutes. The traffic streamed across the piazza, emitting a continuous, syncopated howl. The poor fool wouldn't have thought his life in danger; if the explosion had left him a micro-second to register surprise, he surely would have done so. Everyone – at headquarters, at the Ministry of the Interior, even the prime minister – had known the nature of his mission: a sop to public opinion which, after all, had been only moderately aroused by the assassination of Judge De Angelis which Fabri had been investigating.

So the investigating magistrate's assassination had been a great surprise.

A large tree, resplendent with autumn hues in the late afternoon sunlight, overshadowed the cafe's pavement tables. To Anders, it looked artificial, petrified, in the tranquil afternoon air. The famous plane tree ... still in shock. Abruptly, he turned away, and took a taxi to a small hotel half a block from police headquarters. He did not enter the hotel. When the taxi had disappeared into the traffic, he set off along the street.

Police headquarters was a heavyweight stone structure, its grey facade dripping decorative stucco. It was further despoiled by the excretions of generations of pigeons, and in the last sixty years, of motor cars. Its several hundred windows, deep-set in their elaborate architraves, reflected a turbid sunset back to the street in stabs of reddish light. To some citizens, they seemed like penetrative eyes. Anders, having imagination, had thoughts like that, but today wasn't the occasion for such pleasant diversions. Already he felt tense and isolated, was calculating how long it would take him to do his job and quit the city. Above the building the national flag, with its three broad vertical stripes of green, white and red, hung limply from its flagstaff. Its familiarity gave him no reassurance; everyone knew the regional authorities flew it with deep contempt.

Anders showed his ID, was saluted, passed through a metal detector, was clipped with a colour-coded card, and taken up in a lift to the first floor. He'd opened his suitcase for them; the fact that he was from Rome, the Ministry of the Interior, seemed to make the day of the sergeant at the barrier; there'd been a sly gleam in his eye as he'd riffled through the contents, removed the gun. Anders had borne it patiently.

At this point, the commissioner was the only one in the city who knew of Anders' mission – officially. He kept the inspector waiting only five minutes. A flock of harassed-looking aides exited in a rush from the chief of police's office. Anders stepped aside, then stepped in.

'Ah, Inspector! Welcome.'

Anders approached, shook hands across the desk, and took the chair which the commissioner, who hadn't left his own, indicated.

The commissioner was compact, well made, with a sharply-clipped black moustache, an olive complexion, and slashed and burned patches of skin under brooding, brown eyes which appeared sore. Below his left eye in this rough, a tic pulsed. His black hair was expertly cut – very short, and plastered down with an intrusively aromatic hair oil. His movements were abrupt, as though each thought was a surge of electricity, jolting from him a specific reaction. In short, he shone with grooming, had about him an atmosphere of ulcers.

Anders was not surprised at the evidence of stress. He watched the tic, and was reminded of a frog's heartbeat. He had quite a precise knowledge of the commissioner, though he was confident there was much more to know. Here, ostensibly, was the pillar of law and order in the city. What a lie, what a pity.

The commissioner lit a cigarette. His eyes darted suspiciously at Anders, at his suitcase, lingered on that battered, leather article which had been the length and breadth of Italy. Anders wondered: does he equate me with a travelling salesman about to make his pitch?

The commissioner swiftly disclosed the origin of his suspicion. 'My dear colleague, with respect, why does the Ministry of the Interior, send an officer of ... of ...' He came to a halt, pursing his lips, the cigarette waving in his fingers.

'A mere inspector?' Anders suggested, equably.

The commissioner shook his head impatiently, 'Of your rank, to look into the matter before us. We've seen several high-ranking officers here, and most recently as you know, an investigating magistrate ...'

After another pause, Anders said mildly, 'Who's dead.'

'Regrettably.'

Anders' left hand rested lightly on his suitcase. This visit was protocol — merely a courtesy call to be completed expeditiously. He understood that the commissioner would not have welcomed a more senior officer, but was puzzled and suspicious, perhaps affronted in the queer process of the ego, to have only an inspector on his hands. To allay the man's unease, he supposed he should say something about it.

'And, an officer who ... who ... has ...'

'An artificial leg?' Anders ventured.

The commissioner grimaced, 'who's not, totally, physically fit.'

Deep in his heart Anders sighed. He looked steadily at the chief of police. 'Sir, I don't know the answer. But I surmise my superiors, perhaps even the minister, calculate an officer of my rank is less likely to attract attention — more likely to survive the ... hazards of your city. To carry out this routine task, and depart, intact so to speak, thus not raising the further unwelcome scrutiny of the media, and, of certain troublesome sectors of public opinion. This is merely a guess, of course.'

The commissioner stared at the detective, then shrugged, as though such a notion was ridiculous.

'Naturally, you have my full cooperation. I must

presume you know your business. I won't detain you. Here's the card of one of my officers. He's at your service. Where can you be reached?'

Anders was on his feet, the suitcase in hand. 'I'll let your man know,' he said politely.

The commissioner frowned. He remained seated, puffing at his cigarette, his bloodshot eyes blinking rapidly on Anders' back as he walked to the door. The Rome policeman closed it carefully behind him. The commissioner sensed that the man didn't intend coming back, and it increased his annoyance. He flicked a switch on his console.

'Tell Matucci to get himself up here, fast.'

Anders faced the city again. He was glad to have that over. A gust of wind swirled from nowhere in the street, knocked leaves from the trees. It brought foul factory smells and coal grits from the railway shunting yards. In his state of tension, he took the rush of air as a warning signal. Be alert! He looked up; at least it had lent the national flag a moment of dignity.

Anders had not been frank with the commissioner; he had a better idea of why he'd been selected for the mission than he'd said. There would be very few people whom he could trust in this city, and the chief of police could not be counted among them. He took a taxi for three blocks and alighted at a corner of the municipal gardens which he entered through the famous, century-old iron gates, and walked briskly along the asphalt path. Halfway across the gardens he paused, then sat down on a bench.

The pedestrians following in his wake were trades-men and clerks, shop girls, on their way home. How poor most of them looked, hurrying along in the dregs of the day. Dispirited and wary: there was a little energy in the faces of the young, especially the girls, but the older citizens appeared washed up. Quite understandable in this depressed urban wasteland; though, the judge's widow had spirit, if the media could be believed.

Presently, he moved on, as satisfied as he could be. Taxis waited at a rank on the far side of the park. He took one, directing the driver to the eastern quarter over the river. They moved into the traffic. Ahead in the street, a pair of yellow buses – ramshackle antiques, transfused with cannibalised parts – went tigerishly in tandem through the traffic, farting poisonous fumes. Carelessly, one veered and side-swiped a small overtaking sedan, sending it spinning away onto a median strip. The bus didn't stop. The taxi driver shrugged, growled morosely.

Predictable, Anders observed: the bus line was owned by a firm with links to the mafia. If you wanted to take care of your health, it was a company you didn't sue. And here he was, until today a semi-retired Rome policeman who'd seen his best days, stepping into the mafia's heartland, with about the same degree of per-sonal security as a lamb entering an abattoir. He smiled mirthlessly.

Looking for the address given him by Arduini, a carabinieri colonel and lifetime friend, he walked less smoothly, and with a little pain, along a narrow, rough-cobbled street. He had to search back and forth: eccentric street numbering. Overhead, women taking in washing from a lattice of poles gossiped across airspace exchanging family information, news of husbands' infidelities. The chitchat of the urban ghettoes. On the beat in several cities, he'd heard it all. The suitcase had become heavier. This is hard work for a semi-retired hero, he thought, stepping through a doorway, above which was a lamp and the sign: Bar Carella.

Signora Carella, from behind the bar, stared across her establishment as though she'd expected Anders' appearance in the doorway that very second. Immobile, he stared back. She dropped her eyes, moved two wine glasses a fraction, seemingly embarrassed by his direct look, but in fact, merely thoughtful.

To Anders, Signora Carella was an impressive, stimulating sight. Nearly six feet tall, perhaps forty-five, the hair flicking friskily across her shoulders, she stood behind the bar with the authority of a proprietor, her tightfitting black dress seductively moulding her pendent breasts, prominent stomach.

He put down his suitcase and found his breathing had quickened, and not solely from his exertions in the street. She raised her head: her face had the creamy hue of a gardenia; her eyes, he guessed at this distance, were probably green.

To Signora Carella, Anders was merely an interesting case. He was quite fashionably dressed, not tall, yet not short. His hair was a mixture of black and grey. The face was distinctly authoritative – yet also calm and sympathetic. She judged it an out-of-doors' face, which at some point had become indoors. A northerner … dependable. And what is that dreaming look about?

Fifty, she thought, though age was unimportant to her. Is he the one who has been recommended? And why does he stand in that way?

All patrons who entered her bar attracted such scrutiny. The times, which had dragged on for so long, bred caution in any proprietor. She observed his undisguised sexual appraisal, put no special importance on it — it was something she was exposed to daily. Police? Probably. But of a different kind.

After these few seconds of mutual scrutiny and assessment, Anders took up his suitcase, walked across to the bar, and gave the name of his colleague. Yes, she said, there's a room available to the friend of an old friend like Colonel Arduini. The price was very reasonable; the bar smelt of difficult times. And definitely, green eyes.

Oh yes, carabiniere or somesuch, she decided, as she led the way up the narrow stairs. It squared with the source of the introduction.

Anders guessed what she was thinking, but as he followed he was diverted by her swaying hips centimetres above his face. He watched their easy movement, the muscular, well-shaped (dancer's?) legs, smelt a musky fragrance.

In the small room, after she had gone, he unpacked his suitcase, and placed the few changes of clothes in a closet. He took out an artificial leg, his spare. This was Mark I; he was wearing Mark II. In the ten years since he'd lost his left leg high above the knee, they'd been assiduously improving the technology, and the government had been pleased to keep him abreast of it. He carried a spare on trips, as a man with poor eyesight carries a second set of spectacles. Losing his leg had been a traumatic and bitter experience, but time had converted the bitterness to acceptance, and the wooden leg with its steel innards of working parts was now, if not an old friend, an old acquaintance.

From the bottom of the suitcase he took out another old acquaintance, the worn shoulder-holster with his 9 mm Beretta, which they'd returned to him at police headquarters when he'd exited, and strapped it on with the air of knotting his tie for the ten-thousandth time. It was ten years since it had fired a serious bullet.

He found the bathroom, washed his face and hands, combed his hair, and went down to the bar. Tonight he was in a mood to be diverted; he would have a good meal, a little of the regional wine.

Half a dozen patrons were eating or drinking, and Signora Carella and a young girl in a white apron were busy. He ate a dish of veal and small marrows, cooked in alternate layers with butter and Parmesan cheese, mopping it up with coarse bread, washing it down with a light, fragrant, red wine. He was a connoisseur of ordinary regional food and wine, hadn't had this dish for years. Most enjoyable.

Working men were the customers. They drifted in from the street in their thick, rough clothes, talked guardedly, ate and drank, drifted out; no public conversations, or female companions.

Left to his wine and his thoughts, Anders watched Signora Carella adroitly moving her large body behind the bar, passing the odd remark to a patron, sending an instruction to the girl, shouting to the kitchen. A paucity of electric light kept her face in shadow.

'Dark are their faces/Deep and shadowy their thoughts/ These intriguing women/Dwellers of this wine and sun-soaked earth,' his ancestor, a poet, had written while in another region. The poet had loved many women. But he and his poems were forgotten. Anders was investigating his life and work, was determined to write a book, bring him out from obscurity. This quest, and his women, were like threads of gold in his own grey, pragmatic life with its heavy tarnish of compromise.

At nine the police patrol entered. The modest bar-life froze in its tracks. Anders heard the two ceiling fans slicing air. The two police took their complimentary grappa at the bar, and stared at the patrons. Helmeted, harnessed with submachine guns, pistols, handcuffs, nightsticks, radios, they stood there, creaking in their leather, icons of intimidation. Their cold, suspicious eyes swept the room. They said: Citizens, watch out!

A band of brothers, Anders reflected, gazing into his wine. This region's police force had its rigid factions, its bitter feuds, its vested interests – like all the nation's security agencies – but was rock-solid against outsiders.

He sipped wine, holding it on his tongue for a moment, glanced towards the bar. With all that paraphernalia they had trouble walking, let alone running. But bullets were fast, and readily used against some, and this knowledge tended to paralyse flight. He'd heard that at the police academy here they followed such dogma as: Question: What is better than a fuck? Answer: Squirting a bullet into an anarchist, sir!

Not that there were many anarchists left these days.

11

He did not look up again, but knew they were looking at him, his clothes, his presence in this bar. But they left, and Signora Carella's patrons seemed to exhale in unison. Radios began whistling static in the street, faded away.

What a country! The mellow wine in his mouth, on his palate, he ruminated on just what a country it was. From 1969 to the 1980s, Italy had been torn apart by terrorist activity from both the left and the right. Kidnapping, bombings, assassinations, had been a terrible daily diet. Revolution was in the air, and the thousands of university students had been anti-government, anti-establishment. The leftists had been the most virulent – in particular, the fanatical Red Brigades. He'd worked with units commanded by General Dalla Chiesa to combat them. By '83 they had the terrorists on the run, had broken them into splinter groups. There'd been a few final acts of terror up to '85, then they'd faded out. It'd been a decade and a half of hell. The pursuit, counteractions, and subsequent trials had been a big part of his life. It had cost him his leg, his career. It had cost many lives – including former prime minister Moro's. Eh! What a country!

Eating his dinner, his dark mood had evaporated. Now it was back. The present, not the past. He ruminated on this, talked to himself: 'Don't let it get on top of you. Get it done, and get out. In a month it'll all be behind you for good.' Pragmatic advice. He trusted he could complete his inquiries in two or three days. After all, his superiors expected nothing but a straightforward repetition of what was already on the public record, except from a fresh and respected source. New insights or information were not on the agenda. It was interesting to see that they thought his old fame, medals, commendations, still stood for something. Personally, he'd buried all that long ago.

However, matters of this nature had a habit of becoming less straightforward than intended. Investigating Magistrate Fabri's brief, in regard to the assassinated judge, had been similar. It had never been intended that Fabri should pose a threat. That message had been made clear in the right quarters. Being the man he was, the magistrate would not have come otherwise – he'd never been one to take the slightest risk. Yet he and his bodyguards had finished up as body fragments and blood pools on the pavement at that cafe.

Inexplicable? Perhaps – to some. Anders had seen too much of random factors at work, chaotic forces.

The magistrate's left forearm, his gold watch still attached, had been recovered from a fork of the plane tree. The commissioner's report to the capital had been regretful, and heavyweight in the 'how' and 'when' of the assassination – unhelpful in the 'who' and 'why' of it. Quite understandable. Now Anders was here to form a view for the ministry on the circumstances of the late visiting official's surprising demise.

One of the police had spat on the floor, drawing a furious look from Signora Carella. She'd jammed the cork into the bottle, making it shriek her protest. Her bare, well-fleshed but shapely arms had glowed in the weak light as she raised them to replace the bottle on the shelf.

Admiringly, he took this vision with him up the narrow stairs. When he'd undressed, he sat on the bed and washed and gently dried his stump, chafed after the day's work, applied the ointment. As he did so, thoughts of Signora Carella dropped away. He backtracked, a little. Poor General Dalla Chiesa had been killed with his magistrate wife in Palermo in '82, not by the leftists, but by the mafia. Anders shook his head. Then he pondered whether, in the convoluted ways of his world, something lay behind this mission which he was unaware of; whether he, too, might have been chosen by Fate to be a sacrificial lamb in a state of affairs now running out of everyone's control.

II

TUESDAY MORNING

AT THE FATEFUL cafe opposite the station, Anders waited for the detective whose name was on the card provided by the commissioner. The commissioner had been right; he wished to avoid a return to police headquarters, preferring to meet the man on neutral ground – if such a thing existed in this city. He wasn't deterred by the site of the investigating magistrate's bloody demise a few metres from where he sat. Lightning, so he had been assured, doesn't strike the same place twice.

It was nearly nine, and the open-air section was faintly sunlit, but chilly. He was the sole patron, and almost suspiciously, a waiter in a white apron came out to him. At that moment the detective arrived. He made his way through the tables, tall, wide-shouldered, carrying a little too much weight, late thirties, moving in a jaunty extrovert's walk. He was blond, with brushed-back hair smooth as a waterfall. A thin moustache was traced beneath a long nose, which had been broken at some stage. It enhanced his looks. The ice-blue eyes that met Anders' had a humorous look.

Christ, the Rome investigator thought. What have we got here – a junior Marcello Mastroianni? But tougher. And, he was the sharpest dresser for a cop Anders had set eyes on below the rank of commissioner. Conservative, grey, well-pressed suit which by its cut might've come from Rizzoli, in Rome's Largo Chigi, white shirt, black knitted tie, polished, soft black leather slip-ons. Gold-rimmed spectacles and a wedding ring completed the picture.

'Inspector Anders? I'm Matucci. Former chief inspector, present rank: detective.' The voice was loud, the tone hinted at amusement at such a reversal of fortune. The mobile lips formed a grin, he presented a big white hand with a flourish.

Politely, Anders stood up to shake it. He noted that in the midst of the bravado this cop's eyes took his measure, which was interesting. If fact, the man's total persona was. Quite unexpected.

'Sit down, Matucci, we'll have a cup of coffee. Get to know each other.'

Anders mainly did things by the book. This meeting was another step in the ritual of national and regional police liaison – something to tick off the list and forget. It was unimaginable that they'd give him a man who was not assigned to spy on him at worst, or incompetent and useless to him at best. When you sat across a table from a so-called colleague of one of the police agencies, you had to assume you were dealing with an opponent. Guess who was in the system, who was out, who was on the fence. It put a torpor into investigations.

They ordered coffee and Anders said in his cautious,

courteous way, 'Presumably, you've been briefed on my mission?'

'Yes, Inspector. It's been in this morning's news-papers. You're to re-examine the circumstances of Investigating Magistrate Fabri's murder, interview witnesses, and make a special report to the ministry.'

'Very good. Quite a simple assignment, really. The local report was commendably thorough.' He articulated the lie easily, thinking: the *newspapers*?

'I wish only to interview a handful of people – the key contacts whom the magistrate met. There are a few gaps in that admirable report. Perhaps I can insert a hypothesis, an elaboration or two, to give my superiors and the ministry comfort. Those articles in the national press ... Signora De Angelis' representations, have found a few receptive ears.' He smiled. 'I don't expect to be here more than a few days, or to trouble you, but it'll be a comfort to know that you're around.'

'I'm at your service,' the detective said. 'That's the commissioner's wish. Fullest cooperation.' He grinned at the Rome investigator, indicating that God had spoken. Suddenly he dipped into a pocket, brought out cigarettes, lit up.

Anders sipped his coffee, glanced at the traffic, this morning boisterously tangoing around the piazza. Already the air smelt, tasted of lead. He really had nothing more to say to the local detective. He didn't want a car; that'd make his movements too traceable.

What he'd outlined was what he intended to do, and it should not give the commissioner, or others in the city, any qualms. But, that had also been the intention of

17

Investigating Magistrate Fabri. They were all playing out a game. If this detective had half a brain, he'd know that. Perhaps that was the source of his amusement.

A drinker, Anders decided. Fine broken capillaries made a slight network across the cheekbones of the handsome face. He looked up at the plane tree which overshadowed their table. Its leaves were sailing down.

'On the tenth of July, a nasty outcome for Investigating Magistrate Fabri and his men.'

Matucci, cigarette stuck in the centre of his mouth, shrugged. 'This city has seen plenty of such nastiness. It's like the bad air, with us all the time.'

The smell of exotic tobacco joined that of the strong coffee. Whatever else it was, on this exposed corner, it was a morning for strong odours, Anders thought, and the dapper detective wasn't improving it.

He'd play it out a little before beginning his work. Never be abrupt in these liaisons. The locals could be touchy, though Matucci didn't look that type. Thoughtfully, with his hand, he swept fallen leaves off the table. 'Ex-chief inspector you said, Matucci. That was my own former rank.'

The detective brushed a shred of tobacco from his lip. He laughed boisterously. 'It's a crazy world, eh, Inspector? We're both heading the wrong way. If it wasn't for the commissioner, I'd be out on my arse. As it is, the next time, he threatens to have me directing traffic down in Central.' He shook his head, as if in mock wonder at his situation.

Anders waited. The next time? Was this detective chronically maladroit? He didn't think so. He had a hunch that behind the no-hoper's persona the man might be working out something quite complicated.

'The commissioner's my ex-brother-in-law.' It came as a throwaway line. Genuine, not calculated.

Anders raised his eyebrows, surprised.

'My wife – his favourite sister – died four years ago. Cancer. I looked after her for three years while she was sick.'

Anders glanced at him. 'I'm sorry.'

Matucci shrugged his big shoulders, serious for once, studied the leaves on the table that Anders had missed. 'These things are out of our hands.'

When he looked up, the humour glittered again in his eyes. 'With respect, Inspector, the commissioner gives me the odds and sods to look after. Yesterday afternoon he said to me: 'Here's something for you Matucci, which even you can't *fuck up*.' Eh-eh! You can see how we stand.'

Anders couldn't, the relationship seemed to have complex undertones. He sipped coffee. Matucci was looking at him, obviously waiting for a reciprocal confidence. Why was this Rome investigator an inspector, when with his service, medals, and public record, he should have made much higher rank? An anticipatory grin flickered on the handsome face.

Anders smiled slightly. A carabinieri squad car slithered around the piazza, siren blasting.

'Going to their coffee-break,' Matucci said.

'How are the carabinieri here?' Anders asked, referring to the nation's second police service. Extreme competition and jealousy existed between the rival bodies.

Matucci stubbed out his cigarette. 'As they are everywhere. Always trying to stick their noses in where they aren't wanted. The colonel in charge is a weak bastard. So that handicaps them a bit.'

He patted his pockets, then suddenly rhythmically beat the tabletop with his hands, as though playing bongo drums. 'Eh, Inspector, if that's it, I'll be off. You've got my card.'

Anders was astonished.

Matucci was up. 'By the way, where are you staying?'

'I'll be moving into new accommodation today. Not yet decided. I'll let you know,' Anders lied.

The local detective grinned understandingly, raised a hand in salute, and went off in his jaunty, swaying walk.

Anders watched him go. Did the man think he was a comedian? Or, was there a screw loose? Definitely no screws loose, he thought, remembering the moments when the ice-blue eyes had been steady and assessing. He'd stick with his earlier hunch. Maybe the comedian act was a facade, covering his lost wife, his lost rank. Some men covered up their losses, or their inadequacies, with humour, buffoonery. Or, maybe some more covert agenda. Anyway, he'd never find out. He didn't plan to see Matucci again.

It was time to go to work. He entered the cafe's interior to make a phone call. Several minutes later he left. As he passed the plane tree, he noticed its trunk was embedded with myriad glass fragments, as though set by a jeweller. They sparkled in the autumnal sunshine like diamonds.

On his way in a filthy taxi to the judge's widow's apartment, Anders watched the city go by with a jaundiced eye. He wasn't looking forward to the forthcoming interview — he'd keep it short. He'd read the reports, Signora De Angelis' letters and articles in the press — the few she'd got into print — the headline piece about her, following Investigating Magistrate Fabri's assassination. And her dossier.

All of it had made him feel ashamed. But at this point in his life, dwelling on it would be an indulgence useless to anyone. He wished to get clear of the sordid complications of the service, the nation's life. Retired in '82 on a disability pension, reinstated in '89, now he qualified for a full pension and had applied to retire. He asked only for time to be left for himself — for a testament to his ancestor-poet. To go out, with a cleaner taste in his mouth. Yes, he'd get this interview over quickly.

The taxi drew up before a vast apartment building, dotted with long rows of small windows. It resembled a passenger liner tied up at a wharf. He got out, with the usual slight difficulty, paid off the surly, unshaven driver. Entrance B. That was it. He stood on the pavement, looking up to the third floor windows above the entrance. Had a curtain moved? He looked left and right along the avenue, which was lined by more plane trees.

The liftshaft was in the middle of the stairwell, and he rode up in a metal cage, cracked and stained marble stairs close beside him. Obviously, the common area of the building was unloved. It was dusky and frigid. God knew what it would be like in winter.

Signora De Angelis was not looking forward to this meeting either – anger was her prevailing emotion. She understood its real purpose, the tone that would attach to it, hated the hypocrisy, saw it as yet another insult to her late husband. She walked quickly through the rooms of the large, gloomy apartment, smoking a cigarette, moving in fits and starts, hesitating here and there to nervously straighten this or that. Her heels clattered on the parquet floor. In throaty, contemptuous tones she spoke a few of her thoughts aloud: 'These evil men! Why do they bother with such facades?'

She stopped, drew on her cigarette, visualised the late Investigating Magistrate Fabri in this very room. 'Corrupt fool! He could have stayed at his desk in Rome and written the report. Less trouble. Safer!'

She clattered on, a tall, slim, long-striding woman. The government released such fictions gravely, authoritatively, to the media. Public opinion, that hothouse flower, was stifled. Almost invariably. It was pitiful, how meticulous they were with form and legitimacy in these tasks. Like a careful housewife wrapping her kitchen rubbish, while down the road monumental airborne garbage from factories is dumped on the city, as the politicians stall a clean air ordinance.

She laughed bitterly, briefly. Such is life. And death? It had been close to her for more than a year, circling like a shark, not yet hungry enough, not yet certain of the victim's edibility. Where are you God? Her lips twisted into a grimace of a smile.

The apartment was furnished with fine antique pieces; several tapestries, and a dozen or so excellent oil paintings in elaborate gold frames – mainly of the late judge's ancestors – hung in the rooms. Formerly, the rooms had gleamed with polish, glowed from her ministrations. Now there was a patina of dust over all, and enterprising spiders had trailed their webs from the cornices; books, magazines and newspapers were piled erratically. A computer system purred softly in one room, its blue screen alight but blank – as though temporarily surfeited by input from the surrounding deluge of files, handwritten notes, and news clippings.

The cataclysmic change in Signora De Angelis' life had drastically re-arranged her priorities. Only one corner had escaped the rot – the judge's large, gilded, writing desk. It was orderly and polished; just as he'd left it the Saturday they'd blown him up in his armoured car, en route to the Summit Insurance Inquiry.

She came to rest in the hall. At that moment, the front doorbell sounded. Her slim hand raced to cover her heart.

The force with which the door was flung open startled Anders. Hat in hand, he stared at the woman. He remembered himself, and bowed slightly.

'Good morning, signora. I'm Inspector Anders. Ministry of the Interior.'

'Ha! You're on time.' She waved him in with a tense gesture.

He had seen photographs of her, but in person she looked younger. She was forty-three; the judge had been sixty.

He stood in the drawing room, the brim of his hat in

his hands. 'Signora, I regret this intrusion. Unfortunately, my duty requires it.' He spoke quietly, seeking to defuse her obvious tension.

Signora De Angelis took a few steps, as though inspecting him. 'Ha!' she responded. 'Duty!' Her lips moved with a pronounced emphasis, revealing small, perfect white teeth, too small to be the product of a cosmetic orthodontist. Little dazzling pearls. She became still, her gaze fixed on his face, her brown eyes wider, apparently taking in every detail and blemish.

Fascinated, he watched this scrutiny. Not a good start, but just as he'd expected. She did not remain still for more than a moment. Her nervous energy seemed awash in the room. *He* stood still, looking like an intruder despite his courteous demeanour and attitude. And *feeling* an intruder. He studied her dark face, taut with lines of strain, sprinkled with freckles across the cheekbones. She had an air of the country about her – though her clothes and bearing were of the city.

They both knew who had killed her husband. That she understood perfectly his routine complicity in the arrogant, rough and ready universal lie which protected the system and those responsible for such crimes, or, at least, his total ineffectuality in the face of them, was one source of his discomfort.

'I'll get through this as quickly as I can,' he said, watching her perambulation, his head moving like a spectator at a tennis match.

'Please do,' she flashed at him.

Still in his overcoat (she'd not invited him to remove it) he followed her through the rooms, began asking his

24

questions. She shot answers at him in monosyllables – plainly all he, his questions, deserved.

Apparently, at their interview, Fabri had merely raked over the coals of the original investigation, kept to his checklist. Well, that was to be expected. Just as he was doing, using it to add a gloss of authenticity to his own inquiry. Sad to say. But ordinary men could not work miracles. Extraordinary men had tried, had not succeeded or survived. The wheels driving the nation had continued to turn, pragmatically as ever.

'Ha!' she said, ignoring a question, struck by a thought. 'Look at this!' She went to her desk – they were moving through the room with the computer – and rummaged in the mess, her hair falling over her eyes. Triumphantly, she held up a news cutting, and began to read it rapidly: 'Rome – Monday. Top Investigator to Re-open the De Angelis and Fabri Cases. Inspector DP Anders, one of the nation's most decorated investigators, holder of a Presidential Commendation, has been assigned by the Ministry of the Interior to assess the investigation into the Judge De Angelis and Investigating Magistrate Fabri assassinations. Anders became a public hero in 1982, when his determination, investigatory skills, and personal courage broke The New Dawn leftist group. In the course of that case he was blown up, and lost a leg. He is already in town, and the ministry expects his report within two weeks ...'

Signora De Angelis stopped, out of breath, and flapped the clipping derisively in the air. Ah yes, Anders thought. The ministry's public relations people were preparing the way for his report to go on the public record.

'Well, Inspector?' she said, her head to one side, two paces from him. Her eyes were brown with golden glints, he saw, and he had an intimation that they were trying to stare into his soul. If only they could see all the ins and outs of it! 'If it's true, why do I have the same sad old bell sounding in my heart?'

He said, quietly, 'I do have an artificial leg.'

Why had he said that? He could stand all day if he had to, but preferred to sit and did so now, excusing himself. He sympathised profoundly with this woman, as anyone with a grain of compassion would. And he did feel ashamed. And, he admired her. Her grief was extraordinarily self-centred he judged, and her courage was honed to a hysterical edge, but it was a case worthy of the greatest tolerance. She was anti-mafia personified, and therefore, anti-government. Face to face, he felt he was breathing in her bravery.

There was nothing to be done. No magic wand to be waved. He knew the nation's apparatus of power was impregnable. It was a pity – no, a tragedy. But it was an ironclad fact. And, it was a personal tragedy for this woman that she would never accept it. He felt depressed, but pragmatic. He should complete his questions, and get out.

By sitting down he'd restricted her sporadic movements to a single room, the one with the computer. She paced it, smoking a fresh cigarette, still holding his 'testimonial'. He saw she'd not finished taunting him, the system. 'Be patient,' he told himself. He examined the late judge's photograph in a silver frame: a sepia-toned face, a neat moustache, mole on his left cheek,

26

heavy-lidded, reflective eyes. Not a line, or a hint of humour; sensuous lips. The ornate, gilded desk resembled a shrine. He had seen this kind of thing before. He'd read the judge's dossier, and some things had puzzled him.

'Tell me! What heroism have you been engaged in since 1982, Inspector?' Her voice had deepened, become even more throaty.

Was the throatiness due to her incessant smoking? he wondered. She had stopped in the centre of the room to gaze at him with another intense stare. Impatiently, she flicked the fall of hair from her brow. Doubtless she had always had an exceptional character; her husband's outrageous murder had driven her to the extremity of it, forged an unswerving obsessiveness. From what he'd read about her, was insanity far away?

No answer to that. Here he was, probing at human flesh and nerves – his own brand of obsessiveness. Why not talk to her? He shifted his mind into the new mode.

'Signora, after '82, I was retired for seven years, then came back for part-time duties. Inflation had done its work on my pension.' He did smile, slightly. 'For three years I've been doing retrospectives on unsolved major crimes. Mainly working from the files – a fresh mind, fresh eyes, sifting the toil of the original investigators. Sitting at a desk reading, taking notes, thinking. Perhaps taking a look at the scene. "Work" is hardly the right term. The witnesses, usually, are long gone. Successes have been minimal. Two prosecutions, one conviction. I'm to retire, finally, in a month. Early, my choice.'

He'd revealed to her something of his inner life. What did that signify?

She smiled mockingly. 'So, this is your last assignment. Major crimes? Crimes against the status quo, against vested interests? I think I can see your work, your situation quite clearly, Inspector.'

With a vigorous shrug, Signora De Angelis dismissed it, moved on to a window which projected above the street three floors below. She turned back to confront him, her face even darker against a background of sunlight. Slivers of strained light rained down it continuously like tears – or small arrows-heads. From his sofa, he thought: How extraordinary!

'Ha! The inspecting magistrate was an articulated waxwork. A clothes' dummy. Nothing there but wind and whistle. He cautioned me! "Dear lady," he said, "consider your position. You can achieve nothing but your own ruin." Was that part of his brief, Inspector? Or was he doing some unofficial spadework, being the man of common sense and compassion? Did he fancy his chances with the sexually starved widow? Men from Rome are like that. Don't you agree, Inspector?'

Anders was silent.

Deliberately, she lit yet another cigarette from the one half-smoked. Her movements had become calmer. Perhaps she was tiring. Anders looked across the room to a painting of naked peasant women bathing in a sea grotto, with sailing ships standing off on a hazy horizon. The varnish on it shimmered in patches.

'These bureaucratic hacks,' she said in a softer, clearer voice. 'These frightened men. Concerned for their skins, their fringe benefits, their pensions. I despise them.'

He sighed inwardly. He might have said to her, 'Forgive me, but you speak from a position where almost all has been lost. They have families. They need to survive. It's a question of priorities. Of course, there are also those who are corrupt in the full sense of the word ...'

But he was silent. She was a person who needed to be talked to, to hear the sound of human voices to relieve the thoughts grinding in her brain. But selectively.

'My husband was a *man*. I give thanks every night that I was his wife.'

Still assessing him, she paused. The sad old bell in her head was not quite sounding its familiar tune: an atmosphere about him, this resurrected hero, tempted her, encouraged her, permitted her, to go on ... an idea had formed in her mind.

She took a deep breath. 'Another like him lives in this city, a famous man. Have you heard of the book *Rigor Mortis*, Inspector?'

'I have. Professor Roditi.' It was an exposé of mafia activities published back in the early 1970s. A rare anti-mafia tract, of scholarship and vigour. That the professor had survived was something of an enigma.

She shot him a look.

Anders got up, and walked to the window. He was feeling the absence of coffee. She'd offered none, obviously the niceties no longer figured with her. His leg creaked softly, once. Taking her earlier position, he felt the sun warm his shoulders. Why had she mentioned the octogenarian writer? The book on the nation's dark underbelly had been out of print for twenty years.

29

A remarkable work – clear-sighted, painstakingly researched – the record of evil, pulsing on every page. He could only think of it in the past tense, though he knew it was revered in a few select circles: the left, the intelligentsia, dissidents of this or that stripe, all of them outclassed by the 'system'. The man and his work had been forgotten by the nation at large.

They had exchanged positions. She was on the sofa, at last at rest. He came back to his questions. He got brief answers again; all that he needed. He took no notes. Her immobility was an absolute contrast to her previous frenetic movement. Time to go. He moved out of the sunlight, into the shadows of the room. Her thoughts had taken a new direction, he judged. It struck him that she was studying him now with a fresh intensity. He moved to make one of his deliberate, courteous exits.

She stood up, her mind feeling its way towards a decision, questioning her instinct, fearful of losing the opportunity, fearful of making a deadly mistake. Above her head, two crystals of the fine chandelier pinged together in a current of air.

Quietly she asked, 'Are you married?'

'No.'

'Any family?'

Again, a negative. Everyone has relatives, but for practical purposes it was correct.

She seemed almost sad. 'In this matter – why don't you consider your position?' She spoke with a deadpan intensity, emphasising each word as if it were an arrow being fired into his brain.

He stared at her, would give no answer, but she'd turned away, didn't appear to expect one. However, her eyes followed him as he left.

Going down in the cranky, steel cage of an elevator, he wondered if she was as surprised as he at the final turn of their interview. He knew what she was driving at. He was at the end of his career with not too much to lose. A stale hero following unheroic, manipulated paths. His inertia a habit, conditioned by the practicalities, the overpowering odds. A man who might've done more with his life. *If* he'd had the courage.

Before today she couldn't have known much about him. But somehow, she'd divined his seeds of doubt and self-disgust. 'Why don't you consider your position?' It lingered in his head. Going out to the street, the threat of her infection clung to him like her cigarette smoke. She was dangerous, and in danger, and he found himself disturbed by both qualities.

They'd picked him up. A big car waited in the street. He didn't spare more than a glance at its tinted windows. It was mandatory they'd be staking out her apartment. And by now they would know his program, direct from police headquarters. He brooded while waiting for a taxi. Golden leaves fell past his head in a whispering rain.

Driving through streets steeped in their past, his own began to roll through his head. His service career: 1959 – the Academy; '63 – second-in-charge at a small mountain town in Umbri; '65 – inspector, general branch, at the coastal town of Ancona; '67, detective branch, in the city of Perugia; '69 presidential protection squad; '73 promoted chief inspector, in the *squadra mobile,*

Rome Central; '76 anti–terrorist squad; '82 invalided out to retirement; '89 recalled to special duties, rank of inspector.

There it all was. The bare bones. It seemed to have gone by so quickly.

Emerging from this arid retrospective, he stopped the taxi at a phone booth, and kept it waiting. The booth had been vandalised, the directory gutted, but the number he needed was memorised. A cautious male voice answered immediately. Anders spoke a phrase, then said, 'Do you have anything to report?'

The voice was low, strained. 'They've got your full dossier. They understand why you're here, the terms of reference. Nonetheless, take great care. They're not totally predictable – even to themselves.'

He hung up, and made another call, referring to a list. Then he instructed the driver to go back across the river. The taxidriver was an old man, turning more nervous each moment, having picked up the following car. 'I'll pay you off soon,' Anders said, taking pity, thinking also he would have coffee, and consider further the case of Signora De Angelis – and himself.

III

TUESDAY AFTERNOON

KILLING A LITTLE time, Anders sat at a cafe in
the small piazza opposite the cathedral which, to
his eyes, looked like a mountain of grey rock.
Patches of the stonework were intricate, but the whole
lacked grace. His churchgoing days were a childhood
memory. No regrets on that score.

He lifted his gaze. On the spire, a huge cross, outlined
in blue neon, blazed against a dun-coloured sky. All of it
compounded his depression, his unease. He finished his
coffee abruptly and left.

A narrow, joyless garden lay under the cathedral's
northern wall. He shivered as he walked through it.
From on high, gargoyles leered. The place had an atmosphere of demons barely held at bay. A few women in
black shawls, perhaps sharing his notion, scurried along
the path, heads bowed.

Around a bronze statue a group of about twenty men
and women clustered: elderly, shapeless in unfashionable
overcoats, they were intent on a speaker who, one hand
lightly caressing the statue, stood on its stone base.
Anders, an aficionado of life's intricate interlocking,

wondered if they were embracing the past, to blot out the present. A shaft of light fell on the upturned faces, gilded the folds of skin. Autumn leaves, holding on against the odds until the first wind.

A small shock: he recognised the speaker. Old magazine photographs flicked over in his mind, matched up with the anaemic, foxy face half-hidden by the brushed, shoulder-length, yellowish hair. It was the writer Roditi if his guess was right.

He walked on, just catching the cultured, ironical voice. 'My dear friends, in those days, the powerful took what they wanted, whether property, position, or women ... our friend here is a case in point ... my friends, little has changed.'

So, Anders thought: the mole comes out sometimes. And he's not handing out much consolation.

The archbishop was fastidious with his hospitality, in his manners. Anders was given bitter coffee and a piece of light pastry. The prelate made a point of coming around the magnificent, carved oak desk to sit with his visitor. He was an astute politician, and a noteworthy coward. Twenty years in the job testified to the former, the medical staff at an exclusive clinic to the latter. Two years before he'd faced major surgery, and it had seemed that he might be about to meet his Maker; a startling lack of equanimity in his demeanour had been observed. Anders had read his dossier.

His flock was fearful and repressed, mostly impoverished, generally without hope here in the south – even the middle class were in an economic decline. Only the mafia and those with links to it were flourishing. The archbishop was preoccupied with the restoration of church properties, the per annum return on the diocesan investments, the funding of the missions in Africa, in preserving medieval manuscripts – a model of diligence in these matters.

Anders meditated: neither a good man nor an evil one, just a man like himself bending to the wind, choosing these patently meritorious priorities, closing his mind to the wind's mocking song. Supporting the mafia's political party of choice, the Christian Democrats.

The archbishop's brown and handsome face formed a confident, understanding smile: 'My secretary tells me you wish to talk about poor Fabri.'

Anders nodded. Everything about the archbishop's appearance was immaculate – scrubbed and starched. He made the rich, antique trappings of his room seem vaguely unsanitary.

'Yes, Your Grace. I would be interested to learn what questions he asked at your interview on eighth of July, what answers he received.'

The archbishop put short, plump hands on each cheek, closed his eyes. Anders watched this ... had so much been said?

With great lucidity and seriousness, the archbishop laid out the conversation of four months before. Here, too, the investigating magistrate had followed his brief. Had he been so inclined, Anders could have ticked off the items one by one in his head. Instead, he nodded encouragingly, waited patiently for the prelate to finish.

Of course the archbishop, with his connections,

knew the real purpose of his mission. Together they danced with question and answer over the old ground, glided smoothly through the motions, arrived at Signora De Angelis.

'The dear, sad, misguided woman has become ... strange ... in her bereavement. Although she was ever an intense person. Unfortunately, I believe she has turned away from the church. I hope in time He will wash the bitterness, the delusions from her heart.'

Fairly unlikely, Anders thought.

'And who's responsible for her husband's murder – in your opinion?' He asked this next question almost diffidently.

The churchman was startled, then mesmerised in a defensive silence. His tone, when he replied, expressed polite indignation. He twisted the ring, agitatedly, on his fleshy finger. 'Anarchists – of course! They have not identified themselves, but we know how they work. In this case, their objective might well have been to direct the blame to other quarters. You have great experience of these people, Inspector. You know, their psychology is complex, devious. Virtually unfathomable.'

Anders admired the archbishop's disingenuousness in the face of the unexpected question. *Other quarters?* Who had he in mind? Clearly, he felt absolutely safe from contradiction or challenge. His attitude said plainly: after all, are we not tuned into the same frequency? Acting in concert in the nation's overall interests? Dancing in unison, across this wasteland topic?

On an impulse, knowing he would regret it but unable to restrain himself, Anders said mildly, 'Your

Grace, let me play the devil's advocate. Supposing I was to posit to you that it was not the anarchists who were responsible for the judge's and the investigating magistrate's murders, but another evil influence in this city. What would you say?'

This time the archbishop was rendered speechless. His eyes widened slowly. A slight spasm trembled his brown-spotted hands. It was as though a demon from the roof of the cathedral had entered the room, and perched leeringly on his shoulder. Gradually, his great intelligence wheeled to confront this totally unexpected problem. It bore fruit, in an interrogatory lift of an eyebrow, a cautious pursing of the lips.

He stared at this middle-aged, low-ranking, crippled police officer from Rome with eyes suddenly clouded with doubt and disapprobation.

Anders thought: I've indulged myself, and therein lies danger. Politely, he said, 'Of course, my question is entirely hypothetical. It's my duty to put forward various hypotheses. The record should always have that kind of veracity. Naturally, the ministry, the government, know the anarchists were responsible.'

The archbishop was relieved, and extremely polite at their parting. Nonetheless, the rhythm of their dance had been destroyed.

Walking out of the palazzo, Anders ruminated on the clandestine talks, the plotting, the confessions, which the room he'd just left must have heard over the centuries. How many of the incumbents had betrayed their moral trust like this one? However, he regretted he'd not been able to hold back on that last question. Had the

De Angelis woman thrown him off balance? He shrugged, resolved to watch himself from now on.

He'd not lunched, but the archbishop's delicious pastry floated airily in his stomach. Three more interviews and he'd be finished; the mayor, the banker, and Signora Contrera-Kant. He returned to the same cafe, consulted his list and made two phone calls. He spoke to women secretaries, listened to their discretion and competency oozing down the line in flawless northern accents. Imports. They were expecting his call. The appointments were made. The mayor would see him tonight at 6.00 p.m. – not at the town hall, but at his residence.

He decided to take a grappa, a little cheese and biscuit. The cheese in the region was famous, and he'd been looking forward to some. In Rome he could afford only the second grade. Now he ate the yellow, three-year-old Parmesan slowly, sipped his drink, gazing at a statue of a composer of the eighteenth century in the piazza: a rugged, imposing bronze piece, oxidised slime-green, deep-layered with pigeon shit. The city was crammed with these icons of the marvellous past; no modern statues existed that he knew of.

A tattered man materialised at his table, eyed the cheese, asked for a coin. He gave it. Watching the beggar drift off across the piazza, he dismissed the interview with the archbishop from his mind, instead thought of the octogenarian Roditi.

The sun came out, warmed him. The grappa tingled on his tongue and laid its aromatic fumes into his face. He was nearly there – on the edge of the time he'd reserved for the poet, himself. It stood in his mind, as clean and bright as a white lighthouse on a sundrenched promontory.

His mind continued to drift. Years ago he'd frequently had a panicky dream: still unmarried, no children, and time running out. He no longer had that dream; time had run out.

He ignored the parked car, the hidden watchers. The day now brooded somnolently, a touch of humidity in the air. 'As summer sweetly sighs her last farewell ...'

An hour on his bed at Signora Carella's was an attractive thought. He paid his bill, left the cafe, and again became devious. He quickly lost the car, smiling slightly at the thought of the consternation now replacing boredom behind the tinted glass.

★

Detective Matucci gazed down at the body of the murdered police sergeant. They'd been colleagues in various departments for twenty years. It gave him a jolt to see this man lying there in the street like a piece of garbage. The saturnine face of the corpse, with its toothbrush moustache, halfopen brown eyes fixed on the sky, reminded him of the dusty eyes of a shot hare. The twisted mouth seemed to have frozen in mid-articulation. What last words had been shouted?

Ten metres away two other men, apparently civilians, lay dead. A pistol had fallen near one. They were short, broad men in their thirties, poorly dressed. The torso of each had been torn by a burst of bullets apparently at close range.

The sergeant, obviously, had died instantly. Matucci sighed heavily. His ex-colleague's chest was a mess: blood, raw flesh, bits of leather, strips of soggy fabric, a couple of displaced silver buttons. Heavy destruction. It was hard to imagine that the handguns of the civilians could have produced that effect, but that was what was being suggested.

'Anarchists!' the uniformed inspector, who badly needed a shave, said tersely, confidentially, to Matucci. 'They were attempting to hold up the bank when Liulio came along ... did his duty.'

The radio of one of his men crackled. Matucci glanced at the nearby bank, at flashing blue lights. The police were everywhere, keeping the citizens moving. Eyewitnesses would have long ago quit the scene, hurrying off fearfully with their dangerous knowledge. Later, they might startle spouses or lovers with outbursts from nightmares. Who could blame them? They lived in fear; even an innocent gesture or look might bring down danger.

Matucci turned to a sound of violence. Something fragile shattered on the streetstones. A press photographer was being dragged away between two police. He'd tried covertly to snap the scene close up. A risk-taker, or new in town, the detective thought – either way he was in for an unpleasant session.

The inspector said seriously, 'The mobile patrol arrived a moment too late. He'll get a special commendation.'

Matucci looked at him, as though he'd just heard the speech of the year.

A carabinieri squad car arrived, siren going.

'Christ!' the inspector said disgustedly.

Matucci lit a cigarette and studied the scene. The inspector seemed to be under strain, which was surprising. The police harvested bodies off the streets of their marvellous city daily.

'Eh! Inspector. You're not trying to tell me that those pop-guns did this to our brave colleague's chest, are you? Looks more like a fucking bazooka to me.'

The inspector flushed angrily. 'Listen, Matucci, just do your job, and spare me the crap. Careful you don't get any blood on that lovely suit,' he sneered.

A carabinieri sergeant had arrived. 'I think the detective's got a point,' he said malignantly.

'Mother of God!' the inspector grated, and turned away.

Matucci grinned widely, dropped his cigarette and put a heel on it. He knew there would be no items of much interest on the dead civilians, but he had to go through the formalities. He sucked his teeth, tasted the residue of his last cigarette. Deceit and hypocrisy were in the air. Whatever the story, the dead cop had been a good one.

★

Anders' taxi detoured around the scene of the incident. Through the windscreen he observed the police, the flashing lights of municipal vehicles, the closed-off street. A crime had been perpetrated, or was in progress. A routine sight in his life – in all their lives.

41

Signora Carella's establishment was quiet as the grave when he entered. No-one was in sight, silence flowed out from the slumbering, scrubbed-up kitchen. Softly, careful with his leg, he went up the steep stairs to his room.

★

Soon back in the tiny, partitioned space which was his office, Matucci typed up his preliminary report. He was concise, using numbered paragraphs. His enumerated observations and conclusions were scrupulously correct, as far as they went. The two civilians – convicted anarchists – had escaped from prison that morning. Arming themselves from underground sources, they'd gone after funds. This was an immaculately logical conclusion – though there was one unharmonious aspect. Until today, there hadn't been a single escape from the city's prison in twenty years. Supporting qualification: the law of averages indicated that one was overdue.

This was the report which his superiors expected to receive, but the ancient typewriter clack-clacking in his ears, contrarily hammered out lyrics to a rough tune: two birds with one stone ... two birds ...

A half-smile on his handsome face, he tapped away, his snowy cuffs protected by tubular plastic guards which he'd slipped on. He finished, and whipped the report from the roller. Matucci knew, although it wasn't in his report, that the dead cop had been an undercover agent for the ministry in Rome.

So – this was the opening game with this Inspector

Anders. He doubted if the violent demise of the agent would shock, or even unduly surprise the phlegmatic, strangely polite northern policeman. He leaned back in his chair, and pattered a rhythm on the desk top. What a fucking joke world they lived in!

★

In his room, Anders unstrapped his pistol, removed his left leg, and, seated on the bed, eased off his right shoe, undid his belt, loosened his tie, and lay down on his back. This was a favourite time; relief trickled through his body.

The shutters were closed, but light penetrating their interstices projected a ladder-like pattern on the wall. He let his thoughts run free.

How young in his mind he'd been feeling. It was as though thirty years of his worklife had been peeled away. The period of retirement had done that. During it, he'd progressively shed his ragbag of knowledge – of events and affairs, secret information – his wear and tear. Even the covert contempt had dropped into a kind of hibernation. Returning to his sedentary retrospection of stale cases hadn't changed this much; it was not field-work.

But apparently this state had been an illusion. One hour back on active service the pressure, the contempt, had returned, and he was feeling his age. It seemed the service, its connections and dark experience, would always be there, like a watcher standing back in a door-way.

Hardly surprising, really. And yet, with only four weeks until his final retirement, might not the illusion have survived?

In a house in the narrow street, a clarinet began to play. It sang him, super-sweetly, an unknown melody. A local song? He lifted his head to listen, then let it drop as the sound also fell away into the sluggish afternoon. He had a vision of the player's lips, suddenly frozen, as if at a discursive thought, on the mouthpiece.

The service had been − was − his life. He'd been diligent and determined, he'd tried to do good work circumspectly, cautiously − though he'd taken a minor risk now and then. And here he was, still at it.

He closed his eyes, drifted on to other subjects.

Yesterday, today, the young, nubile daughters of the city striding along with their firm, uplifted breasts, traces of confidence and hope still on their smooth faces, had not aroused him. Though he was pleased to observe them, they were not his heart's desire. It was some among their mothers, aunts, grandmothers who quickened his blood: his appetites, physical and intellectual, were for experienced, life-weary women, adrift from their former moorings. He loved their lived-in lives, their quiet fortitude or desperate vivacity − as much as their bodies with their pendent breasts, and soft, protruding stomachs. The numberless divorcees, widows, spinsters, the unhappily married, had offered him a plenitude of cases.

In a way, his pursuit of these women was the comedy act in his life. He'd no doubt those who knew of his tastes saw him as an eccentric, ridiculous character. He lived his professional and personal lives cautiously, diligently, introspectively. With these affairs of the heart, an individual with a very different character seemed to co-exist in his skin.

Signora Carella he'd recognised immediately as a classic of the type. Where was she at this moment? Lying heavily, quietly, on her bed? His instinct suggested there was no man in her life at present.

Like the promise of an affair, a breeze wafted across the sedated city, into the room. Pleasantly he drifted into sleep.

At 5.00 p.m. he harnessed up, did his hair, and came down to the bar to telephone. The girl was setting tables. He dialled the memorised number. A delay, then the receiver was lifted and he heard a measured breathing. He said nothing, and hung up.

Thoughtfully, he ordered some red wine. The evening paper was on the bar, and the face of the murdered police sergeant stared up at him. He read the article and laid the paper down. The eyes in the photograph seemed to speak to him regretfully: 'It was always a matter of time.'

He sipped his wine, began to quieten down. How many times had he needed to absorb similar news?

Signora Carella appeared behind the bar. Anders turned to look, glad of the distraction. She had washed her hair; gleaming and still damp, it was plastered to her head. Tonight she had put on bright red lipstick. The low candlelight electric bulbs (as proscribed by the power-short region) permitted a sickly illumination – but the skin of her face, chest, and arms glowed. It reminded him of paintings in ill-maintained regional art galleries: obscure, with rays of light beaming down to irradiate a face, a patch of skin.

She wore a green blouse, generously opened. He regarded the wonderful show; felt hopeful that it was for him, felt a constriction in his breathing. She nodded to him, her green eyes lambent, yet essentially unreadable. He said, 'I'll return for dinner about seven-thirty,' and received another brief nod.

Signora Carella watched him go, and talked to herself. 'Where are you off to my mysterious friend? To business which is dangerous? Take care. For a man like you, this city is as sharp as a cut-throat razor. But perhaps you're used to danger. I think so. Yet, you're a different kind. You blue-eyed man with the foreign name. But you're Italian. Yes, a rare one, certainly, in the life of yours truly.'

In the ice-breezy street, walking away, Anders ruminated: definitely like a gardenia. And the look wasn't a discouragement.

IV

TUESDAY NIGHT

SIGNORA DE ANGELIS prepared her frugal dinner, a delicate yet fortifying soup. The recipe had been in her family for over two hundred years, according to her grandmother. 'Strength and determination!' These days, when her energy and will flagged, the soup was one of the stimulants she forced on her herself – a memory of country life from her childhood.

Nervously but deftly she sliced capsicum, and considered the northern policeman. Was she grasping at straws? As their meeting had progressed, an instinctive feeling had risen in her about him – tenuous, nonetheless there: a man above the ordinary.

The fax line rang, startling her. She put down her knife and hastened in. The machine was whispering out a stream of paper. She ripped off a section. His dossier! She'd been waiting on this, hoping ... She put her hand on her heart. Thank God! Here was the gift of a risk-taking wellwisher in Rome.

She scanned the lines of print. Interesting career, interesting story – though so much would be missing. She paused, here and there, her slender finger marking a spot, going on. By God, here was something! Two old incidents buried deep, glinting like nuggets of gold in an overburden of silt. She read with intense concentration, rising excitement. She'd been right! The final section fell from her fingers. She lit a cigarette with trembling hands, stared starkly at a distant point beyond the judge's desk. How had he kept it under wraps? Perhaps they'd been seen as aberrations, or their nature was discernible only to one with special insight.

Was there really a chance? Small surges of confidence and doubt alternated in her mind. Abruptly, tears smarted in her eyes. She didn't know how she'd survived the past year, how she would the time ahead. She returned to the kitchen, walking quietly.

The vegetables were in the broth, slowly heating.

The question was: had that core in him withered and died? Would any appeal be met with caution and indifference? Worse, would it prompt betrayal?

She weighed in turn the likelihood of her perception, the seriousness in him, the traces of honour – how far an official dossier could be trusted. Doubt turned over in her mind. She stirred the soup; steam rose into her face.

Outside in the darkness a few cars sidled past, tyres slithering over a skin of wet leaves.

And the other factor? Despite her distracted state she had noted his unabashed, assessing eyes on her body, her mouth. Hardly noteworthy, accustomed as she was to men with sexual pleas in their eyes. Investigating Magistrate Fabri had looked at her with crudely camouflaged lust. She knew investigators' eyes, womanisers' eyes. But the eyes of this inspector?

She ladled the soup into a bowl, carried it to the kitchen table. The only certainty was the dark stream down which her life was hurling. She would confront him! Seize the opportunity! If she was wrong, and it took her down, so be it. She stared into the soup, as she had into the future and the shadows, beyond the judge's desk.

The intricate problem of getting a message to him, suddenly was occupying her mind. Where was he tonight? She began to eat the soup.

★

In the heart of an undistinguished, ill-maintained stone building in the old city, the commissioner was having one of his less comfortable meetings. He was in mufti, having driven himself through the darkness in a small private car.

The four-storey building was built of rough-faced, dark-green basaltic stone. A stone-paved courtyard served as a parking lot for cars; it had a semi-decrepit fountain. Tonight, the wind was playing havoc with its antique sprays.

Its facades looked upon two minor streets; on the northern side, a tunnel-like gate gave access to the courtyard; no windows on the ground floor faced the streets, and those on the first floor were covered with ugly wrought-iron screens. No brass plates, no signage at all showed at the entrance.

The building was as anonymous as its architecture, which suited its purpose: for many years, it had been used by the mafia for various functions, including administration.

The man called Algo faced the commissioner across a writing desk which had been made for Napoleon Bonaparte. The desk was clear except for one item – a dossier. His hands lay one in the other, still as a stone carving. The hands were manicured, and he was groomed to perfection: his dark suit beautifully made, snowy shirt, gold cufflinks glinting, tie umber-coloured, richly patterned. He was in concord with the room, which resembled a richly chased jewel box in a dungeon – he was perhaps even a trifle more perfect than it. As though acknowledging that possibility, his narrow white face showed a dry amusement. His large, brown eyes regarded the chief of police with the benevolent look of a mentor. However, his thin, hooked nose suggested a bird of prey.

He tapped the dossier from Rome. 'Interesting reading. This inspector's led a full life.'

The commissioner leaned forward, said carefully, 'He's had a long period of service.'

'Excellent work against the Red Brigades in the seventies and early eighties.'

'Yes. If any one man broke the New Dawn group, he did.'

'Of course, much of what's here is a mishmash of reports by different hands at different periods. But I find a unifying thread running through it. Certain nuances. Unfortunately – unfavourable ones. With a record like this, such a pity.'

Smoking was forbidden. The commissioner's brown hands twitched. He didn't know what Algo was referring

50

to, but he had no doubt that the top mafioso's subtle, fertile mind would detect hidden meanings if any were there to be found. All he knew was that obtaining the dossier had caused him difficulty. Things were changing – in Rome, at least.

'Actually, dangerous nuances. And there's our dear archbishop's report, straightforward until we get to the devil's advocate question, if I may so term it. Here, the man revealed himself in a flash. Though quickly he dissembled, withdrew into the shadows, so to speak. Also, he's aware of our surveillance, and when he chooses, avoids it. Why? There are two negative possibilities: his mission to our city may be more complicated than we've been led to believe, or he may have a personal agenda. Either way, he must be regarded with suspicion. We don't wish to have another incident at this time if it can be avoided. But, it might not be avoidable.'

The commissioner flinched. 'May I suggest a degree of circumspection? The investigating magistrate's case has proved extraordinarily troublesome. This inspector's here because of it. There's a lesson to be learned. But you know my opinion. And you've seen the outcry. It was an unnecessary step.'

In the chief of police's mind, 'unnecessary' could well have been substituted with 'incomprehensible'.

'My dear Commissioner, I do. I have.' The white hands unfroze to rise in a slight levitation from the desk. 'In any large organisation events occur which are not totally controllable, incidents of an aberrant nature.'

The commissioner said, 'That may have occurred to our northern visitor, his actions may merely be a protective response. If there is to be another incident, please use your great influence to avoid a bomb. Carnage in the streets is never good public policy.'

He was being as forthright as he judged prudent. The commissioner had known several of the very top mafia bosses. Algo, with his polished manners, his intellectual pursuits, was a hell of a lot different from them. And he was a lot smarter, and a lot more dangerous.

The other nodded slowly. The investigating magistrate's assassination had been an act, doubtless, rooted in convoluted ambitions, which he expected to unravel and deal with. The commissioner would have made his guesses about it. He wondered what they were.

'Anything else known about him – not in here?'

The commissioner said, 'His sex life is active – with somewhat eccentric tastes.' He explained a little.

Algo pursed his lips, was silent. The commissioner waited. The conversation, in the beautiful room, seemed to have drifted to an inconclusive close.

Algo sighed. 'Well, Commissioner, can you enlighten me on the death this afternoon of that undercover Roman policeman you've been giving your hospitality to all these years?'

The commissioner could not conceal his surprise. If any enlightenment was to come, he'd assumed it would be from this extremely dangerous, narrow-faced man opposite, who was taunting him with those sardonic brown eyes which, as usual, put his own to flight.

★

Anders had left Signora Carella's at 5.30 p.m. He walked to the corner, and hailed a taxi. To reduce the cab's stench of cigarette smoke he wound down the window; from the back seat he watched the taciturn, blue-jawed driver spear belligerently into the wheeling waves of traffic. Half the streetlights were turned off for reasons of economy: weaving, flaring, bobbing carlights provided the main illumination in the decaying asphalt arteries; the citizens afoot were reduced to jittering, rat-like shadows.

Tomorrow night, hopefully, he could quit the city – certainly by the following day. He'd made no notes on the two interviews so far, needed none to write the report the ministry expected. He stared grimly at the darkened streets.

You were most at risk when you thought you were safe. The death of their man underlined that. The sergeant had been undercover in the region's police for ten undisturbed years. Now he was a local hero, his death the subject of lies in the evening newspaper. Daily, this city's venal editors went on performing their barefaced distortions, unchallenged and unchecked. For some of them it was a question of commerce, for others, survival.

Anders had not known the man personally, however he felt a valedictory sense of comradeship. But for his presence here, the sergeant might still be alive. It was a notion he chose not to dwell on.

The taxi swerved out of the traffic, jolted through a web of slummy sidestreets. A sweet, heavy smell suffused the air. They passed a soup cannery. A giant sign portraying a rich, ripe tomato glowed in the darkness, a still-life for the proletariat. Walls thick with anti-government graffiti drifted by under the headlights: silent screams of protest from the young. This displayed a degree of courage, given the harsh penalties. Although, the kids could dive into their holes faster than rats.

The mayor's official residence was in a better neighbourhood. A row of palazzi drifted by, well back behind iron-railed fences, with stone-flagged forecourts studded with fountains and big, bronze Baroque vases. Like pale ghosts, guard dogs loped around the grounds. This street was well illuminated, the mayoral residence floodlit. High on the house, which had once been a ducal palazzo, the city's standard drifted in the evening breeze. Anders alighted from the taxi beside a small guard-house. He breathed, smelt no soup here. Three police stood at the gate, watching him stonily. This'll be interesting, Anders thought.

He produced his identification card to the sergeant, who took it suspiciously, became deferential, and saluted. He consulted a clipboard, made a note.

'You're expected, Inspector.' He hesitated. 'Excuse me sir, there are some regulations ...' He moved his hands in an explanatory gesture.

'Naturally.'

Embarrassed but committed, the sergeant stepped forward, began to run his hands lightly over Anders' body. He halted abruptly, as he made contact with the artificial complexities within the blue serge material of the left trouser leg.

Anders, smiling, said quietly, 'A gift from the terrorists.'

The sergeant looked relieved. 'Ah, my sincere commiserations!'

He found the holstered pistol, paused again, then stepped back slowly. Anders watched his face, the thought transparent on it. He was young, clearly had not encountered this situation before. Police from Rome were not frequent visitors here. Obviously, no-one could enter the mayoral residence with a gun. On the other hand, one did not lightly seek to relieve a superior officer — an officer attached to the Ministry of the Interior — of his personal weapon. A more experienced sergeant would have handled it with polite arrogance, and some pleasure — reflecting the historical tension between the two agencies.

They regarded each other. Anders waited patiently. The two junior colleagues observed their sergeant's dilemma with interest.

Anders relented. 'Perhaps, you would be good enough to keep it for me?' he inquired politely.

The sergeant's relief was manifest. 'With pleasure, sir!' He escorted Anders to the front door, past another two police who stood there, to avoid any further inconvenience.

A long line of the city's mayors had found it easy to tap into municipal funds, and one result was the opulence of the mayoral residence. Anders was confronted by a soaring marble staircase; he looked left, right, observed glittering chandeliers waltzing away down splendid, interconnecting rooms. Apparently preparing for a reception, numerous liveried servants hurried about with trays of liquor and canapes.

Mayor Salvo received him in a room on the first floor. He was short but broad, with brushed-back hair that shone like Japanese lacquer. His eyes had the same kind of shine as he stood, legs apart, in the centre of the room, balanced like a motionless hunting cat, watching the Rome investigator's approach. He wore a dinner suit, and had an outsize diamond and gold ring on a hairy, bony finger.

'Inspector! What an honour! Welcome to our city. Congratulations on your fine record. Come and sit down. Here, is comfortable. I know of your sacrifice.'

Anders bowed slightly, shook the hand that had been thrust forward with a theatrical flourish and took the chair indicated.

He'd been curious to meet Salvo. In the nation's corners of dissent and resistance, he was regarded as an icon of municipal maladministration. It was said, usually surreptitiously if the speaker was prudent, that in this he'd surpassed his formidable predecessors. Confident, ruthless, corrupt: that was Salvo's record. Officials in this city were untouchable by the police agencies. The only possible danger had been from the terrorists, but they'd been wiped out in the eighties.

Comfortably seated, Anders wasn't surprised to observe a man who did not even to a minor degree appear to match his reputation. Unlike the elite of the mafia, these municipal officials were often charming and personable. Anders had thirty years' experience of the type. This man's manner was as polished as a prime piece of the region's subtly-veined marble. It was quite astonishing, when you recalled his murderous past.

56

Eyes like tiny, glittering mirrors. Anders thought: Lean close enough, and you'll see your face in them. He sighed internally. A municipal crook at the top of the pyramid – no more than that. Dangerous, but in varying degrees, weren't they all?

Sleek head inclined courteously, attentively, towards the northern policeman, the mayor settled himself, waited for the questions. His attitude said plainly: I'm at your complete disposal. He was fully alert, not under-rating this little chore. Anders, as he prepared to go into his routine, smelt an expensive fragrance. The mayor related his conversation with the investigating magistrate: it was entirely predictable. Unlike the archbishop, he didn't presume that Anders was there to dance with him over preordained ground.

The mayor had had the benefit of a briefing on that interview, and he played his cards differently. His attitude and remarks were quintessentially polite, but completely neutral, assuming nothing. Probably this investigator's terms of reference, the outcome of his inquiries, would be as they expected – but there had been that warning signal.

'We discussed the Futuris Motorway,' Mayor Salvo said. 'A wonderful project. For the region. Though it's had its critics. The poor misguided judge was critical of it at the inquiry. Seemed impelled to cast a wide net over our city's affairs. One always walks a fine line with a major project. The outlay is terrific, and there are, in all such cases, quite legitimate alternative claims for the deployment of the financial resources. One must have a sense of vision. Find the right priorities. Serve the community's longterm interests. One takes the best advice. Weighs it. Hopefully reaches the right decision. A great responsibility.'

Anders nodded gravely at this load of claptrap. The archbishop was intelligent and perceptive, but the mayor was streetwise. Entirely to be expected – he knew he was being watched for a wrong move. It appeared 'the devil's advocate' remark had been a costly indulgence – and in reality, an aberration, for Anders' report would not give the various interested parties in this city any qualms.

The mayor continued his spiel on his civic good works with bright, counterfeit sincerity. Running this city was a great challenge, a great trial, he said. This morning, he'd been horrified to learn that during the night, rats had eaten the fruit off a bedside table in a suite of their premier hotel. 'Can you believe it?' His horrified utterance appeared a genuine reaction.

Anders only half-listened. He'd gone a long way back – to the tenement quarter of Ancona, and was for the hundredth time going up narrow stairs to the third floor of a building, pistol in hand, to try to talk a murderer into surrendering. Below in the street, a hushed crowd and his colleagues waited. The man had seemed amenable, then suddenly had fired, creasing Anders' scalp. In a reflex, Anders had shot him dead. He'd received a mayoral commendation – from a man who might have been this one's brother.

The whole nation knew that the Futuris Motorway was one of the most ridiculous, arrantly corrupt projects in living memory. It serviced no particular need; it was a motorway to nowhere, the critics whispered, merely a conduit to put vast sums into the pockets of politicians, city officials, favoured contractors, and of course the mafia.

Anders didn't waste time on this civic obscenity – it wasn't in his brief – though obviously, it was prominent in the mayor's thoughts. Instead, he asked the stock question.

'I never look for simple explanations,' the mayor said with a charming smile. 'Human affairs are complicated, but I've been obliged, in the cases of Judge De Angelis and Investigating Magistrate Fabri, to reach one. The murders were the work of the anarchists. Both cases. That, certainly, was Fabri's view concerning the judge's death. The evidence is ironclad.'

Anders nodded. Salvo had at last come out of the neutral corner. It was interesting to hear him say 'murders'. And, what 'evidence' was he referring to?

'A new group?' Anders inquired.

'I fear, yes. Who knows better than you? That sort of thing is very hard to isolate in the early days. Eventually, we uncover them.'

Anders recalled that Salvo's predecessor but one had been killed by terrorists. Blown up in his box at the opera, together with his wife and guests. The fact had not been reported in the media, but the former mayor's head, trailing bloody tendrils, had shot like a cannonball to the back stalls, and landed in someone's lap. The eyes had been popped out like burst grapes.

'And Signora De Angelis' views, her campaign?'

The mayor shook his head. An expression of earnest

regret settled on his face. 'Ah ... grief can be an insidious taskmaster, Inspector — a secret poisoner. The balance of the poor woman's mind ...' He uttered these last words with a lingering intonation, and gave a shrug which sought eloquently to convey his opinion, and his compassion.

The formalities were done, possibly recorded on some hidden device, Anders thought with equanimity as he took his leave. Mayor Salvo's eyes, on the detective's back as he left the room, were calculating. The mayor was considering how this policeman had escaped the honoured society's attention for so long. Probably, his seven-year stint in the anti-terrorist squad had quarantined him from the nation's normal business activities, which the mafia bestrode. But what was he up to now? Something was not quite right.

Descending the marble staircase into the bustling atmosphere of the imminent reception, Anders, step by step, pondered the opposing forces at work in the nation. A bleak notion evolved: a graph charting the forces of justice would be like his unfortunate country's international balance of payments, substantially in the red ... yes. He visualised an economist's chart, conscripted for this purpose, the plunging red line.

It would be interesting to submit the analogy to Mayor Salvo. Probably, the bastard wouldn't bat an eyelid.

A scrap of paper — the maidservant who opened the front door for him had pressed it into his hand. He slipped it in his pocket, retrieved his pistol from the sergeant of police, holstered it, and patted the fall of his coat.

On the next corner, his mafia shadow, a long, stylish Mercedes, decorated the almost empty street like a piece of modern art. Anders smiled slightly. Given its occupants: black art. This ancient district could chew up and spit out such modern trifles any time it chose.

He was not in a mood to welcome clandestine messages. They might insert complications into this mission, which he wished to keep in its straitjacket, might even oblige him to delay his departure in order to maintain the charade of the investigation's veracity. He wanted to be done with this rotten assignment.

His annoyance continued to fester; it was all so bleak – and useless. And he was hungry, wanted his dinner, and before he could have it would need to devote time and energy to losing these watchers – assuming there was flesh and blood behind the tinted windows. Therefore, for the moment, he ignored the note.

A young man cruised innocently past on a Vespa. A bearded, swarthy man in a dark-green weathercoat, wearing white sneakers. Too innocently? And was that a suggestion of a weapon, ridged across his chest, under the coat? Anders was inclined to trust his judgment. The young man gazed at the mayoral residence, disappeared into the darkness. Another mysterious fragment in this city's mad mosaic.

A taxi came. Anders eased himself into the rear seat, heard the dark car start up. He failed to observe another car, small and nondescript, waiting in a side street.

Thirty minutes later, he entered Signora Carella's bar. He

checked the company: similar patrons to the previous evening, he recognised some. The police were in situ, arrogantly breasting the bar. They turned their moody, intrusive eyes on him. The owner also breasted the bar. She shot him a look of some complexity.

Anders went to a corner table, studied the menu, ignoring the police scrutiny with the air of an innocently preoccupied citizen. Presently they departed with the usual commotion, fixing the patrons with final, correctional stares. We cops can't help it, Anders reflected. We typecast ourselves; just like the municipal garbage collectors working at the run.

The girl came, and he ordered *bomba di riso*, pigeons in rice, and selected a bottle of vintage Scorza Amara – a red wine as dark as it was powerful. It was expensive, but what the devil. He wished to raise his spirits tonight – and to make a gesture towards Signora Carella's profits.

These days, during solitary meals, he tended to daydream; if he was drinking, the dreams were often exuberant. Normally they did not relate to his day-to-day existence, but to romanticised and amusing flights in a more heroic life, wherein he delighted the hearts of the longlost sweethearts of his youth. Not to be taken seriously.

But of late, his thoughts turned more often to the research he was doing on the life and works of his ancestor-poet; this was serious. He took that direction tonight, considering the mystery of a lost year – most of 1871 – when the poet had gone missing. His forebears had been going missing for centuries. The first one

Anders knew of had come to Rome nearly two centuries ago from the Netherlands. He'd stayed long enough to marry and start a family, then had disappeared to 'the spice islands'. Maybe Indonesia. His family had never heard from him again. A man on the move.

The bottle was nearly empty. The wine coasted warmly down his throat, picking up the residual taste of the meal. He abandoned the missing year for the moment. His stump was chafed, painful, tonight.

The patrons ebbed away to the cold streets. The girl, a silver crucifix swinging between her lemon-sized breasts, a less than devotional expression on her face, cleared his table. He looked at her again.

'I don't know how you get away with it,' Arduini had once said to him. 'The way you conduct yourself can only be defined as sexist.'

Anders had smiled, but not replied. His women were his soulmates. Recognition of what could be shared had always been instinctive between the parties. That was the way it was. There were marvellous exchanges with some, with others it was merely pleasant. He valued them all.

A woman in a northern town had sent him a packet of sixteen letters, smelling faintly of herbs, tied with a black ribbon: the poet's letters written in 1867, to the woman's great-grandmother. The love affair had lasted twelve years, he knew; the letters covered six months.

Signora Carella, abruptly, stood over him and his discursive thoughts. He'd found out her first name was Cinzia. Now, the green eyes were intense. She held another bottle of the vintage wine. 'With my compliments,' she said. He stood up, pulling out a chair.

Her room was a good size, as was her bed. Reclining on it, she watched him undress. Efficiently, unhurriedly, he removed the pistol and harness, the artificial leg, swung his right leg onto the bed. He felt warm and content from the best wine he'd had in years, and, from what he imagined was ahead.

When he'd first set eyes on her, Cinzia's loneliness had been palpable. It had been in the air, as they sat over that second bottle of wine. It was in her fine, penetrative green eyes. It was in her voice, as she'd stopped him ordering a third bottle. The bar had turned chilly as the temperature of the autumn night dropped. But he'd felt warm, his face flushed.

Inches from his face in the dark room: the luminescence of her skin, the creaminess of the gardenia. This close, the light out, he held the rest of the vision in his memory: the thin-boned aquiline nose, the long drop and swell of her breasts, the fan-like, black spread of hair on the pillow.

'Does it still give you trouble?' she asked, her hand on his thigh.

'A little. Not too bad.'

'Are you police?'

He nodded. 'Broadly speaking, Cinzia. But not for long.'

'Broadly,' she repeated, and 'not for long,' as though they were the answers she'd expected.

'I'm retiring. Are you married, Cinzia?'

'Pah! He disappeared ten years ago. Left me with debts, and no happy memories.'

Their lips met in a first, joyful, unhurried kiss.

In perfect unison, they moved languorously, for incalculable periods. Her long, soulful sighs caressed him in the darkness as much as her hands; her tongue roamed in and out of his mouth; her mouth against his throat breathed the sighs into his skin. Under his hands her ample warm flesh had a muscular tone. The years had only moderately diminished his vigour – though now it was not manifested in repetitions, but in endurance. Throughout the night, into the early hours, they ascended and descended 'the hills and valleys of their passion'. He seemed to be drawing closer to the poet each day. Was his ancestor in his secret place watching him now?

Once, momentarily unbalanced by his disability, he tobogganed on their perspiration off her generous stomach, and she laughed quietly, deliciously.

Slow freight, stopping here and there, going on. This was his kind of poetry.

V

WEDNESDAY MORNING

BEFORE DAWN, Anders awoke. His mind felt as smooth as a desert sandhill – so did his body. The day ahead might not be so smooth – might have a different shape from what he'd planned. Last night he'd read the note passed to him at Mayor Salvo's. *'Please meet me 10.00 a.m. at Bar Messico. Be discreet. D.'* A vision of that lady waking to her own grey dawn, to a renewal of fevered thoughts, to fear, came to him like a figure emerging from mist. Here he was, in the bed of one fabulous woman, thinking of another of dissimilar, but also wonderful calibre! Despite his perturbation he found he had an erection.

Propped on an elbow he looked out through the half-open shutters. A grey cold dawn. Fog. Municipal vehicles groaned in the distance, like large predators on the prowl. Cinzia turned to him again, and they made love with the familiarity and affection of twenty-year lovers. This night would have a special incandescence in his memory. There was a wondrous light in the green eyes, from which sleep had fled. 'O, dear Mother of God,' she breathed.

At 8.00 a.m., he went downstairs to the bar. His vexations of the previous evening came back: Detective Matucci sat at a table, newspaper spread open, aromatic cigarette in hand. He lifted his carefully-barbered head, his ice-blue eyes, to the footsteps on the stairs.

'Eh, Inspector. It's me all right.' He closed the paper.

Anders sat down at the table. 'How did you do it? More to the point, why?'

'How? I followed you from the mayor's residence. Quite illuminating – your technique. But I know this town. Too much for the other side, though. They've had their own way too long. Rough and ready, overconfident.'

'I see.'

'As for the "why" – Inspector, that's a longer story.'

Anders turned to look for the young girl, saw her approaching. 'What's your name?' he asked.

'Rosetta, sir.'

'Bring me ham and eggs and coffee, my dear,' he said, smiling. He felt immeasurably closer to this establishment. From the gleam in the girl's eye, he saw that the establishment felt closer to him, too.

'Sweetheart, bring me another coffee,' Matucci said to her, winking playfully.

She departed, face suddenly ablush. Anders nodded to the other to continue. He didn't especially wish to hear what the detective had to say, he doubted whether it would be helpful to his assignment, or in his personal interest, but he'd been tracked down, and the man hadn't done that for no reason. His ex-brother-in-law, the commissioner, must be applying pressure.

The detective said, 'Regrettably, we in the local police have a dead colleague on our hands. No doubt it's come to your attention. The terrorists struck again yesterday. That's the conclusion in the report I've filed. The official version.' His handsome face lit up in a wide grin. 'Round here, that means barefaced lying.'

Anders was surprised at the remark. He nodded slowly, smelt the cooking begin. Cinzia had arrived in the kitchen. Was her face still soft and relaxed from their lovemaking?

'Inspector, the actual whys and wherefores of it are hard to explain – logically. In that sense, the murder resembles the investigating magistrate's.'

He pulled out his cigarettes, lit up, his fair hair bent over the flare of the match. His glance flicked past the policeman from Rome, appraising features of the bar with curiosity. He'd picked up Anders' proprietorial mood. 'Of course, he was one of yours. Had been for ten years, and, it was no secret. I hesitate to say it – but, respectfully, his killing … seems to have been triggered by your arrival.'

Anders showed no reaction, said nothing. 'The official version' accurately expressed the frequently futile, corrupted nature of their work. Nothing new there, but this dapper, offbeat detective was trying to weave some kind of pattern for him, trying to set up a point of departure for somewhere. In fact, making an unexpected play. Surprising.

Obdurately, he resisted it. He watched the detective cast a glance out to the bleakly autumnal street. Was he getting to the point? 'An officer in my position should be embarrassed. But who gives a stuff about that! Nonetheless, I'm your liaison link, and when the commissioner asks your whereabouts, what you're up to, I've no information beyond what's common knowledge. "For Christ's sake, Matucci," he says to me, "get off your arse and find out what he's up to!" He really loves me, but he can't help himself. Your formal appointments, naturally, are well known within a select circle. It's worrying certain people, that you take pains to avoid surveillance. If your mission is as the ministry has carefully conveyed, they ask: "Why is it so? Is there a hidden agenda?" *A Hidden Agenda.* Every bastard's favourite phrase in this city.'

With a comprehensive shrug which summarised the mystification of these shadowy powers, he butted his cigarette. 'Inspector, you won't be surprised to know your dossier's materialised here. They're confused by you. With Investigating Magistrate Fabri there were no such worries ... and *he* was killed. So you'll appreciate your situation is ticklish ... On a knife edge, I'd say.' He grinned at this refinement. 'But then, I suppose you always knew that.'

Anders sighed to himself: my rare, small indulgences buried in thirty years' activity – until a certain kind of mind puts it under the microscope.

Detective Matucci was allowing Anders to look into his mind. Or so it seemed. It wouldn't be unreasonable to expect him to be an agent provocateur, but he still didn't strike Anders like that. So what was *his* agenda? Maybe the debonair, failed detective was a brave man. Maybe he was anti-mafia, maybe a leftist.

So what! Steadily, unproductively, Anders regarded the misty street through the front window. His thoughts seemed to be proceeding along lines as straight and cold as the city's tramtracks – to wind up in that mist.

Obviously, he was giving out conflicting signals. The note in his pocket tended to confirm it. He was there to do the job as specified, as warranted. He would make no waves; they need have no fears. His evasions were the acts of a cautious man, who took into account the illogicality of incidents such as the murders of the investigating magistrate, the undercover police sergeant. And the indulgences? Long in the past. But try explaining that to them ... damn the archbishop! Irritably he dropped a hand on the table.

'How did it go with the mayor?' Matucci asked.

'Much as expected.'

Matucci nodded. 'A viper of a man. A charming viper. His latest piece of nastiness surpasses his usual standard.'

'Oh?'

'Two months ago he had his private secretary killed. A complaisant enough young fellow, who for some queer reason decided to blow the whistle on a corrupt deal. Hard to know which one it was. Or why he did it. He wasn't so stupid as to do it here. He went to the capital, but unfortunately spoke to the wrong people. They picked him up when he arrived back on the night express. Took him to a farmhouse, beat him to a pulp, cut off his testicles, and shot him through the back of the neck.

'It goes further. Next day, the mayor called on the

young widow in his official limousine full of flowers. A beautiful, simple young woman. Eh! you can picture it. Charm turned on, counterfeit sympathy, the works. Her parents stunned by the power. He seduced her later, made her his mistress. She wouldn't have had a clue what was happening. Now, according to her frantic parents, she's disappeared.'

'A nice little story of our times,' Anders commented.

'Eh–eh! Inspector, you're right. Isn't it good to be alive?'

Anders grunted, began to think about the day ahead. Frowning, he looked up as the ham and eggs arrived, and their coffee.

'Did the archbishop break any new ground?' Matucci asked.

Anders put a good sprinkle of pepper on his eggs. This detective was needling away in his offhand manner. Why aren't you shutting him up? 'New ground? Not a concept he'd have in mind in regard to this investigation is it?' He spoke shortly.

Matucci drew on his cigarette, not discouraged. 'He put twenty millions of the church funds into Summit Insurance. Got them out days before the crash. The church commissioners must've thought him a miracle-worker, with a direct line to the Almighty. The Summit's pension-holders didn't think so. Inspector, I know who I'd put my money on.' He laughed, reflecting on that event.

Anders knew of this. Judge De Angelis had got the archbishop into the witness box at the inquiry – made him dance a fast and intricate dance with the truth.

The detective said with a sudden intense bitterness, 'The question is – will truth and justice ever be stronger than the mafia, than the politicians, the bureaucrats in their pockets, not to mention the business types? Than the damned web that holds them all together? Are good men, with balls, going to be endlessly slaughtered like sacrificial lambs. Eh! Inspector, who can give us the answer?'

He regarded Anders over the rim of his coffee cup, silent at last.

Anders was eating, did not respond. Did not show that he'd even heard the little speech. What was this apparent bravery in aid of? What did Matucci hope to achieve with talk like this?

Anders left the bar. Why was he going to this meeting? No sensible answer. For the first time, he had the feeling that he was being drawn into a tidal-race. Fog still blotted out the far ends of the streets. The taxi quickstepped around the piazza next to the station, peeled off into a minor street. He began looking for a sign. He scrutinised the following traffic.

'Here!' he instructed.

Under a stone archway, climbing steps, he went. The steps were broad and shallow, gave him no trouble. He'd destroyed the note. 'Be discreet.' A *milk and water* phrase, from a woman for whom the threat of violent death was ever present. Part of the methodology of her survival?

She was waiting for him at a table in the bar, dressed in black slacks, sweater, leather carcoat, and a hat with upturned brim; badges of widowhood, or camouflage for slipping incognito through the opaque morning? He looked down at her haunted face.

'Good! You're here!' She spoke brusquely, offering her hand.

Anders smiled cautiously as he sat down. Out came her cigarettes, he produced his lighter, these days used only for ladies. He nodded at the interior room of the small bar. 'Tucked away place. A favourite?'

She shrugged quickly, nervously. 'I've never been here.'

He nodded his understanding. How white and shining were the small, regular teeth, revealed by the exaggerated articulation of her lips. She was wringing every possible nuance from each word. 'I believe I was successfully discreet,' he said. A touch of humour might break down the tension. However, she was deeply beyond such subtleties, such trifles. Her eyes seemed cloudy this morning, but they regarded him steadily. They struck him as an anchor among the nervous mannerisms.

'I've read your dossier,' she said.

Another surprise. These dossiers, so much a part of the nation's life, were like timebombs ticking away.

He said, 'A dusty record.'

'I make no apology. Sympathisers in sensitive positions, timely information, are two of our few defences.

He shrugged. *Our.* There it was again. What kind of group was she hooked up to? Had to be from the past, now a sideline to her manic crusade. He thought back to *her* dossier. Coffee was brought. The bar, without other customers, was as confidential as a cave.

With somewhat more care, Signora De Angelis seemed to be walking a similar path to Detective Matucci. He shifted uneasily: he hadn't intended to see either of them again, now he'd seen them both.

'It's a curious record, Inspector. I graduated in psychology. It has many shades of grey, but here and there, a glint of light.'

'They have it.'

'Oh? Yes – of course, they would have.'

'I've never seen it myself. Strange isn't it?'

She gave him a hard, analysing look, ignored his remark. 'How much is conscious, how much unconscious – whether it's all one or the other – would take several conversations and your cooperation, for me to understand. Perhaps in your own heart the answer's not clear. You sit there, showing nothing except caution and an air of reluctance to be present.'

She paused, drew emphatically on her cigarette. 'Whether you like it or not, Inspector, you are present and correct in our nation's affairs. Have you come to this meeting because of your conscience? Or because of your undoubted diligence? I don't think so. It runs deeper than that. I've classed you as a sympathiser, at least.'

She let her head drop, so that the hair fell over her face like a blind. Her breath, her cigarette smoke in his face, he remained silent, as each prepared statement fell on his ears, kept an eye on the door, the street.

A minute earlier, down the street, he'd seen a large man move back into a doorway.

'Listen! I bore my very few friends, people I trust, with a little speech. Listen! The nation, this region, mock the individual. My husband was a hero. Once he'd decided what he should do, he abandoned subterfuge. The Summit Insurance Inquiry was the catalyst. He decided it would be his collision course. He was the *only* official in this city battering on the walls of the mafia, the system, while they pissed on him from the battlements. It was a deliberate sacrifice, he wished to burn it into the record. Not a religious man, and he was afraid. Very afraid. He had his idea ... of the future. He revered the few brave men. Chinnici. Others. He wished to join them.'

Anders sipped his coffee, listening, but meditative. Chinnici was the Palermo chief prosecutor killed in '83 by the mafia. There had been other heroes in this particular war. He watched the fascinating movement of her lips, the sensuous ripples of articulation in the slender, brown throat: hearing what he had to hear, breathing in the danger.

The dead judge, doubtless, would be a star in Roditi's next book — if one was in progress, and if it ever appeared.

One part of him was concentrating on the street.

Signora De Angelis raised her head, flicked back the hair. Her eyebrows shot up. In her low, throaty, intense voice she said, 'And you? Are fifty, have no family, a career at its end. A lifetime of service — of a kind — behind you. A public hero ... who it must be admitted, has bravely served the establishment which he loathes. And yet ... a man who has dissented, but who has dribbled out his dissent in minor acts over a lifetime. What is to be made of that? What is next? Do you retire to the

76

garden, the golf course, the long lunch and the after-noon sleep? Is that the sum of it all? Or – and this is exciting – is the bravura act to come? A single act? To give worth and shape to a life?'

So there it was! He was to smash the mould of his existence! To go into the full public glare with a dissenting report. To write his own death warrant!

In thirty years, naturally, a few close colleagues had observed his 'small indulgences', guessed what lay behind them, had shrugged and, decently silent, gone their ways. The fingers of this woman, with skill and instinct, had found that hibernating pulse.

What a coup! To turn *their* public hero, *their* man, back upon them as whistleblower!

'In the execution it's very simple,' she said, very quietly. 'All you need do, is tell the truth.'

The truth, he repeated to himself.

He studied the tabletop. She held her cigarette, as though she'd forgotten it was in her fingers. He should leave. The smell of coffee wafted in the room. The foggy morning waited.

'Well, Inspector?'

Politely, he studied her face, absorbed the brazen conviction, the electricity of her tension. A starkly beautiful face. No makeup today, and the freckles across her cheekbones stood out like tiny beacons. The judge must have been a driven man indeed to've decided to give up this. But, had he ever seen this side of her?

Anders did not attempt to deny the accuracy of her perception, her diagnosis. 'You seem to expect a miracle. It would achieve nothing.'

'Every stand we make, every point we fight for is a victory.' She bit her lip, swayed in her chair as though momentarily faint, recovered.

'Signora, you must forgive me for being a realist in these matters.'

She gave a short, bitter laugh, sat back abruptly.

And I sit silent, Anders thought, conditioned by the odds, drugged by the hopelessness. Why had so much of his life been spent facing fanatics? He gazed through the window, resisting the manipulation.

The doorway was twenty metres away, and the watcher was still there.

He turned his head back, and had a small shock: the brown eyes steadfastly on him were bright with tears, not tears of helplessness or surrender, he judged instantly, but bitter tears, under control. He understood, suddenly, that the other current in him also had been divined – that an offer was there, as part of a compact. He turned away, marvelling at this, stared down the street at the doorway where the mafia thug, or the police agent, take your pick, was keeping watch. Fog in the streets, fog in his brain.

Suddenly, the fog dissipated, as if in a whiff of breeze. He was out in the clear.

It seemed simple – almost inevitable. The time had come, just as, over the years, he'd sometimes thought that one day it might. He met her eyes again. She hadn't moved a centimetre. He might have been looking at a photograph of her taken those few moments ago. He placed his hand on the edge of the table.

'Signora, I will do what you wish.'

Her shoulders slumped. The cigarette fell from her

fingers on the table. She put her slim hand over her heart. 'My God!' she breathed.

Anders stared, fascinated. Her eyes, in a marvellous quicksilver transition, had become radiant; yellow specks danced in them. The tears were gone, recalled only by the stains on her cheeks.

Then he came down to earth. Imperceptibly, he shook his head, wondering at the force of her expectations. Bitter experience showed that in their sad country, whistleblowers rarely achieved anything more than their own destruction.

★

Alone in his office, on a secure phone, the commissioner listened to Mayor Salvo. The pain of his ulcer brought slight twitches to the corners of his mouth. The mayor had phoned on two matters: the increasing number of beggars who were infesting the city's public places, giving the city an undesirable image, and, Inspector Anders.

He suggested that the police send out a fleet of vans, collect the beggars, take them to the city's outskirts and dump them. The long walk back might give them pause for thought, a roughing-up might aid the process.

The commissioner made noncommittal sounds and waited. What this would achieve wasn't clear to him. And what alternative lifestyle for the beggars did the mayor have in mind? Was his civic colleague going to get on to the rats? Another infestation in the city. The mayor hated rats. He'd an unlimited budget for extermination. But no ...

'Maybe, he's as they claim, this Rome cop. But he has an air about him of private thoughts. A disingenuous operator. Overtly respectful. But I must say, my sixth sense says: a hidden agenda – his own, or his masters'. He's been devious about his domicile here. But it's been found out.' (He gave it to the commissioner.) 'My own view is that action should be taken. I think you should be prepared.'

The commissioner politely acknowledged the comment. Such a decision would not be the mayor's or his.

The mayor said, 'There is another matter ...' He went on to question the adequacy of the mayoral security arrangements.

The commissioner sighed to himself, but listened patiently. It was a matter which frequently exercised the mayor's mind, despite the large security detachment provided by the city. Doubtless, when you considered the number of enemies Mayor Salvo had accumulated ...

After the mayor rang off, the commissioner sat like a statue in his big leather chair, staring at the oak-panelling on the wall opposite. It was his nightmare that all those 'actions' down the years, with which he'd been actively or passively associated, were being collated by mysterious observers, input into a computerised data bank, and would erupt, one day, like a volcano.

He reached for his cigarettes, thoughtfully tapped one on the pack. It was impracticable that any such spy network, or data bank could exist, given the zeal of the special agencies under his control – not to mention the organisation's security apparatus. His fear, really, lay elsewhere: in long, private sessions of reasoning he'd concluded with a dead seriousness that God ran the universe by a system of giant computers, and it was *that* data bank, *that* kind of volcano which, increasingly, he had in mind. One day, he might try out this notion on the archbishop. It would put the bastard into a spin.

He sucked nicotine into his lungs. It was out of his hands — whatever was decided. The tic under his eye fluttered on his skin like a butterfly. As usual, his role would be to pick up the pieces.

★

Across the street from the town hall, the Vespa was parked with a covey of others. The bearded young man loitered on a nearby ledge, reading a newspaper. It had been raining, but now it had stopped. His green weathercoat was turned up around his throat, raindrops glittered in his wiry hair. Occasionally, he glanced at the archway to the town hall's courtyard, checking for signs of unusual activity. The police guard talked among themselves, and fiddled with their submachine guns. He looked up to the windows of the mayoral suite, and his eyes became implacable. It was true — those who hated Mayor Salvo were many, but none more so than the family whom the bearded young man represented. The mayor did not give many opportunities, but in time, he'd deliver one.

After a moment, he lowered his gaze, and went back to the football pages. You needed to be patient in life, he reflected. His team had not won a match this season, but eventually they'd come good.

VI

WEDNESDAY NOON

THEY LEFT the cafe by a back entrance. He doubted if it fooled anyone, but it got them away without a confrontation – though, he doubted if that was intended. Signora De Angelis disappeared, striding away into the fog, and he took a taxi to the Provincial Bank, and his penultimate appointment.

Travelling downtown, he was still getting to grips with the decision. It was remarkable how, in one hour, he'd abandoned the careful patterns of a lifetime, to put himself into this kind of hazard. Signora De Angelis had turned her professional skills, persuasive talents, her fascinating persona on him to the full. And, her fanaticism. He'd be salvaging his selfrespect, she'd said; retiring, a soldier, against corrupt and evil forces. Retiring! What a euphemism for his likely fate. He was too set in his character for that line to cut any ice; something else had gone 'click' in his brain.

He dropped it. Logic and rationality didn't seem relevant. Up a side street, he glimpsed the cathedral's high cross branded against the soiled sky.

He wished to keep his brain clear, but insistently, the

poet entered it, and he picked up the trail of his thoughts from the bar last night. Anton Anders had become visible again at the end of 1871. Suddenly, he'd reappeared in a mountain town in Umbria. He'd rented a villa and begun gardening in a serious way. The slopes of a hillside had been terraced, an orange grove planted. Each morning he'd gardened and watered, each night he'd written. *The Night Serpent*, a sequence of fifty sonnets, had been written there in 1872. His best work. Who was the woman in his life at the time? Anders' research had discovered nothing on this point.

With a jerk, he surfaced to the downtown street with its glass towers slanting skywards; the taxi had darted into the kerb. Implacably, he was slotted back into the grey and ominous present. Outside the Provincial Bank, a ragged man with a desperate, cadaverous face, drooping moustaches, and long breeze-ruffled hair, grasped a placard. It said: *Justice for the Policy-Holders of Summit Insurance.* Obdurately he stared at passersby, pitiful in his solitary defiance. Anders passed him, entered the building of soaring glass and structural granite, and walked over marble. Across the street, he noted a dark-green BMW sitting in a no-parking zone.

Behind, a commotion broke out. He stopped, turned. Two police had arrived. They'd torn the placard from the man and were flailing him around the legs with their long clubs. He danced like a scarecrow in the wind, mouth articulating frantically, moustaches flopping.

A routine incident, sad to say. Anders turned away. He was confronted by a security checkpoint. His appointment was verified on a computer screen. Once again, he volunteered to deposit his gun with the head of security, and was clipped with a plastic ID. Under escort he rode up in an elevator.

On the twentieth floor a lush, expensive silence reigned. He sank into deep leather, and watched secretaries resembling fashion models sweep by, smelt their exotic fragrances, heard phones purr like satisfied cats. President Chiro Rasto, the bank's head, was in conference. The Rastos were household names in the city, and this one, since the crash of Summit Insurance, especially so. The man outside the bank was probably the representative of the several thousand ruined policyholders.

From Judge De Angelis' inquiry, the facts of the debacle were well known, and had featured briefly in the national press until the judge's murder had cut it short. Chiro Rasto was also president of the Summit Insurance group. Unwise real estate investments by his family companies, allied with a failing manufacturing empire, had led to mysterious conflagrations in two major plants, with substantial claims overtaking Summit Insurance. It was well known that the mafia had a stake in his enterprises.

'Acts of God,' Rasto had gravely announced on television.

The insurance group did not have sufficient reserves, or adequate re-insurance; also, it was engaged in some of the same unwise investments as the Rastos – and unfortunately, it was at the end of the line. The Rastos got their money, while the Summit's thousands of annuity-holders lost their pensions.

Even in this city, there'd been a public outcry. The

authorities, slightly discommoded, had set up the judicial inquiry. It was to be a controlled whitewash. Judge De Angelis, an insignificant jurist who'd been passed over for promotion numerous times, had been named to head it. The inference was that if he handled himself correctly, promotion would no longer be elusive. But apparently the judge had been brooding away in recent times, and his ambition had turned into another channel. A channel which had soon alarmed various powerful figures, Rasto at their head, and ultimately sealed his fate. The judge's going off the rails like this had been unpredictable. No-one understood why he'd done it. Anders speculated that he might've had a slow-growing but mortal cancer, known only to him and his medico. Maybe a lot of things. It didn't matter now.

From her fiercely partisan viewpoint, Signora De Angelis had claimed it as his cataclysmic moment – a courageous and effective anti-mafia, anti-government strike. His bid for the nation's attention, and in the event, his own posthumous reputation.

At any rate – day by day in that last week, as the evidence was heard, his interventions had become more probing, his commentaries more incisive. His courage and determination had risen, along with his exhilaration, according to his wife. He was squaring up against tremendous odds. Amazing facts were being mined, stockpiled.

The local press had been deadly silent, but one editor in Rome had begun to run reports, then editorials. Against all expectations, the region's underbelly was being ripped open like a sardine can. Overpoweringly, the stench of endemic corruption was suddenly in the air. The truth-starved citizens had been spellbound.

On the Saturday at the end of that week, Judge De Angelis had been blown up in his armoured car. Under another more reliable judge, the inquiry, likewise, had subsequently crashed to a standstill. Signora De Angelis, a month later, still in her widow's weeds, had come out into the open, and commenced her crusade.

Leaning over Anders and his thoughts, one of the secretary-fashion models, was telling him the president would see him now. What a lovely voice. He stood up, creaking a little.

The Rastos had been transplanted from the north seventy years ago, bringing capital, and their avarice, to turn them loose in a less sophisticated, more brutal environment. The brutality suited them. They'd bred prolifically, importing spouses from the north to order, though the men frequently took the earthy southern women as mistresses. Chiro was the current head of the clan.

And here he is, Anders thought, having to peer quite a way down the room to see him. Immovable behind his desk, Rasto watched the investigator approach. In some of his features, he was the epitome of the rich banker: broad, pale face, soft flowing jowls hanging like expensive drapes, silvery fine hair, glittering eyeglasses, black coat, grey, striped trousers, an air of solid wealth.

'Sit down,' he said. Anders had arrived at the desk, had bowed slightly.

'Anders, attached to the Ministry of the Interior, from —'

'Christ, I know who you are, where you're from, why you're here. Or why they say you're here. Make it quick.'

The investigator smiled politely. Doubtless this heap of excrement was giving his customary warm welcome.

'Concerning Investigating Magistrate Fabri ...'

'Jesus! That weak bastard ... where do you dumb northerners dredge them up from?'

Anders sat back comfortably in the chair. Face to face, his expectations were realised. For years, mainly out of curiosity, he'd run a secret dossier on this man, had destroyed it on his earlier retirement from the service. Despite the sneer, he guessed that Rasto ate northern food, had northern furnishings in his house, liked to play the northerner. But it didn't come off; too much of the south had been assimilated, and his physique didn't assist the illusion. His torso was massive, as though a hunk of the region's basalt lay beneath the banker's uniform – his hands, giant paws sprouting thickets of black hairs, suggested both constructive and destructive qualities. He couldn't disguise his natural air of menace.

Anders ignored the question, and put his hat on the desk, which had nothing else on it but the president's blurred reflection. 'The ministry wishes to review the investigation of the circumstances of Fabri's murder. In its way, it's also a retrospective on Judge De Angelis' murder.'

A truculent frown creased Rasto's broad, white brow. He brooded on the hat, then suddenly lunged forward and swept it off the desk.

Anders ignored that, too. 'Sir, if you'll bear with me, I do have a few questions ...'

Inwardly, he sighed: the last interview but one. However, no longer did it mean an escape into a final retirement and anonymity. He felt a flutter of excitement. When had he last felt that?

Anders didn't deviate from the checklist. Certainly Rasto had been briefed on the nature of his mission, and on the course of yesterday's interviews with the archbishop, and the mayor. Maybe they'd even been listening in to the one with Signora De Angelis. Rasto responded with a contemptuous economy. Almost certainly, he was one of those who'd ordered De Angelis' killing.

Anders neither needed, nor would get anything, from this man. Signora De Angelis would supply the hard information for his dissenting report.

A mucous-like substance was squeezing out between the heavy lids of Rasto's eyes, clogging the eyelids. Fascinated, Anders wondered fancifully if this was an excretion of evil. Then the banker blinked and the glittering black eyes were clear again, and boring into the investigator.

'Sir, did Magistrate Fabri asked your opinion on responsibility?'

'Christ, all who live in this city *know* it was the anarchists. Unlike some shitty editors in the capital who think they know better. My house's a fortress, as is this office. I travel in an armoured car with escorts. All men of influence in our city are obliged to live like this.' He glowered at Anders.

Anders' face was expressionless. The same old line. The world knew that the Red Brigades were extinct, or inactive, at least. The protective measures mentioned were a charade – though perhaps they really feared that new groups might rise from the ashes.

'That's also the ministry's conclusion,' Anders said mildly, 'but of course, verification is needed. Hence the mission of the investigating magistrate, and my own. However, Signora De Angelis' claims have created problems –'

'That deranged woman,' the banker said with furious emphasis. 'She's as crazy as her damned husband.' He meshed his brutal fingers, and cracked knuckles. Then he considered for a moment, quietened down. 'One regrets her situation, but cannot forgive her manic outbursts.'

The room contained a score of green, shiny-leafed plants; vast modern paintings from fashionable foreign artists were spotlit on the walls. Glancing around as though to check his whereabouts, Anders thought of the dark, regional canvases in the De Angelis' apartment.

He retrieved his hat and left. He doubted Rasto would ever be levered from his bastion of power, although merely entertaining the possibility was heart-warming. Perhaps a prayer for a coronary occlusion might do the trick? If he'd been a praying man …

★

Tommaso Bugno gazed down into the street from his room in a building in the city's southern quarter. A powerfully-built man in a steel-grey suit, the material of which shimmered when he moved, he was absolutely still, lost in thought, his back turned on the two big men who stood respectfully in the centre of the room, as though they'd halted on some invisible line. One had craggy features, as white and blank as an empty page, while the other luxuriated in an oiled, swarthy complexion, pockmarked in patches, no more expressive than his colleague.

It was too quiet today. Bugno thought: What is that tunnel-arse Algo up to? What's he going to spring on us tomorrow tonight? The big boss was finished – he'd known that for months, and others in the organisation must, by now, be making up their minds on it. The crisis couldn't be postponed much longer. Algo was playing for time. Doubtless, manipulating his own agenda into place.

Bugno thought: The poncy bastard still has a grip of fucking steel on us. But it's not quite as strong or tenacious. Not since the assassination of the fucking investigating magistrate. We got under his guard with that. Made him look bad. And certain whispers've been put out against him. And now, this Rome cop comes along ...

The delay in grasping that thistle had opened up another opportunity to undercut his authority. For a man who could move quickly, Bugno thought, his brow dark with imminent violence ... In the visiting cop's presence and actions there was a hidden agenda – dangerous. Clear as the cathedral's cross in the sky. For the man who could unravel it, destroy it – perhaps the prize ... As for the De Angelis bitch – why delay?

He could feel the coming power in his hands, in his brain. But he'd have to tear Algo's heart out by the roots to have it.

Decisively, he turned to the two men of his family, who watched his face carefully. He'd spent a fortune on soundproofing his suite, had it swept once a day at irregular times for bugs, but reticence was ingrained in his character.

He said thickly, 'Go ahead, immediately, both of them. Take the cop to the freezer and leave him there. I'll be there at three. Then the other job.'

The two men left, walking heavily but quietly.

★

Anders came down in the lift, surrendered his plastic ID clip and reclaimed his gun. He stepped out onto the pavement, glanced at his watch: a minute past noon. He had an hour to wait for the final appointment, in another glass tower, fifty metres along the street.

For a few moments, his back to the BMW still across the street, he watched the limousines pulling into the bank's side entrance, the entry to the safe-deposit, and observed wealthy citizens, Rasto's 'men of influence', hurrying to covert transactions in their secret world. In this city of the long, black Mercedes, and the capacious safe-deposit box.

It was dangerous to be seen watching this kind of activity. He turned away, went to a bar a short distance along the street, and entered its unpretentious door. The place was an extremely narrow, dark cavern panelled with smoke-varnished wood, badly lit by twin rows of amber-coloured wall lights. Two men were arguing volubly at a zinc-surfaced bar to one side; the investigator guessed they were the proprietors.

The two swarthy, shirt-sleeved men ignored Anders, who went past them to the rear and sat down at a large round table covered with a white cloth. He listened as he passed them. They were accusing, and counteraccusing each other, of taking from the bar supplies.

Anders undid his overcoat. A waiter appeared, giving him an arrogant, angry look when he ordered only coffee. The look plainly said: Why are you sitting at this premium table, instead of at the bar? Because I am, Anders said to himself.

It was like being in a mine-drive looking out at an oblong of daylight. He stirred his coffee, and the BMW rolled into view, rocked to a standstill. Sticking close today. He reached in his pocket for a cigarette and remembered he'd given them up. Chiro Rasto still loomed large in his thoughts: the hard eyes, the atmosphere of corruption and menace. Forget him! He was checked off the list of his confidential appointments, which were about as confidential as the TV news.

He'd been holding it at bay, but now he felt fear closing in; a cold compulsion to get out, cut and run for Rome, or a safe house and his report writing. But any attempt to abandon his scheduled program might sound an alarm, trigger an immediate response. Steady, he whispered. Keep them uncertain. At five o'clock he was to meet Signora De Angelis again – then the final phase would start. He sipped coffee, replenished his courage, his wariness. The coffee in this region was addictive. Like the women.

Now the proprietors were arguing about the payroll,

gesturing to the harvest bounty painted on the vaulted ceiling; they were finding it hard to achieve a meeting of minds.

Mayor Salvo's face imposed itself on Anders' consciousness. The urbane official was smiling, slightly wolfishly, from the front page of a newspaper spread on the next table: a giant photograph – appropriate to the status in this society of a monumental crook. A kind of Red Riding Hood grandma smile, but the wolf's ears peeked out. He was cutting a ribbon with outsize scissors. The caption said: Official Opening of Third Stage of the Futuris Motorway.

Anders gazed down the corridor-bar. He reflected that the motorway had seven more stages to go.

Signora De Angelis. The poet intoned, in some cell of his brain: *'On a perilous journey/Think not of a lady/Watch the deepest shadows/Ease your sword in its scabbard ...'* Too true. He watched the street through the plateglass window. Two men in black suits had alighted from the BMW and were walking towards the bar.

Anders watched them come. He sucked his underlip gently, thoughtfully. Unobtrusively, he took the Beretta from its holster, put it with his right hand into his lap under the tablecloth, eased off the safety. It seemed that the conundrum of his status might be about to become clear.

They stepped into the bar, and stood inside the door, staring into the gloom. The proprietors at the bar stopped in mid-argument. The newcomers' eyes found Anders, and, keeping a few paces apart from each other, they came up the corridor. Big men in their forties, one of portly muscle, with a fleshy, oiled-looking face, the other wide in the shoulders and narrow in the waist, with a milk-coloured, cadaverous face.

The proprietors, silent spectators, twisted their necks to follow their progress. Anders remained immobile. His coffee cup was in his left hand, half way to his lips; it might have been a studied position. He observed that they were both sweating; it sparkled in the amber lights' glow, on their brows. That was interesting. It was a cold day. Mafia gangsters did not sweat over assignments like this; the power and the odds were always on their side and these men would have long and tempered track records.

They pulled out chairs, put their weight down solidly into them. Despite the sweat, the offhand arrogance was impregnated in them as unequivocally as the cigarette smoke into the cafe's woodwork.

Across the white cloth, coffee cup still in midair, Anders surveyed the two faces. He said, 'Good afternoon. What can I do for you?'

'You can get yourself up and come with us,' one said tersely. 'Someone wants to talk to you.'

'Oh? *Someone?*' Anders said, and paused. 'A police inspector attached to the Ministry of the Interior requires more specific invitations than that, to obtain a claim on his time.

The first man took out a handkerchief, and wiped sweat from his brow, angry at having to do it. 'One such is a fly on the wall to the someone I speak of,' he said contemptuously. 'Get yourself up, or we'll lend you some assistance.'

Anders supposed that they thought it quite normal for a one-legged man to be also one-handed. He put down the suspended coffee cup gently, as though it were porcelain. 'No, that doesn't fit my schedule.'

'Don't make it harder than it has to be.' The moisture on the man's face had appeared again immediately.

Anders smiled slightly. 'This someone you speak of, my friends, has put you on something of a slippery slope. You should take time off to think about that.'

The first man breathed out forcefully and the odour of garlic came across the table; his eyes shifted fractionally to his colleague, who hadn't moved a muscle.

'Keep your hands on the table,' Anders said.

His arm moved under the table, and he tapped gently but audibly with the pistol barrel on the wood.

'Hear that? It's a Beretta, 9 mm Brigadier eight shot magazine; friend of mine for a long time. It's aimed at your nuts. With that amount of firepower, not too much trouble to shoot them off.'

Their eyes were all locked in a communal appraisal. He thought: They're wondering if I'd do it. He'd got through to the two proprietors, though. They'd dived behind the bar.

These thugs were mafia – but not strictly on the honoured society's business, he'd guessed, and that seemed to be their sweat-inducing dilemma. He was sure of it now. A renegade agenda; the blowing-up of the investigating magistrate came to mind. The killing of the undercover sergeant ...

They stood up, gazing at him as though he were a puzzle. He said, with mild authority, 'Turn around slowly, and go out. Keep your hands away from your bodies. I've been a B grade marksman all my life, you will know, I can drop you easily at this range.'

Go in peace, he thought. That would be a rare experience for them; just as a confrontation with an outcome like this was. On the whole, they had handled it fairly well.

He sat there over the dregs of his coffee for another half hour, having to put up with the proprietors' harsh whispers and covert glances. They'd be paying protection to the organisation, and would have experience of enforcers. He meditated on his immediate future. A sleek rat hastened along a wall towards the rear, and presumably to the kitchen. It cut into his thinking, reminded him of his sojourn in Ancona. His flat had been infested. He'd had a notion that foreign rats coming ashore had somehow identified his place as a waterfront hotel; he'd trapped them at night, and each morning carried two down to the garbage by tails which felt as hard as braided steel.

These days, he would have expected the byplay just completed to have made him feel tired; but he didn't feel tired. Instead, he considered how hard it would be to get out of this coffin-like bar, and wondered why he'd entered it so easily.

The BMW had driven slowly off to his left. Now another vehicle drifted in, and took up station. Change of shift. A change in the status of his hazard? Could be. Events seemed to be jittering around him like whirling shadows on a windy night.

VII

WEDNESDAY AFTERNOON

ANDERS HAD ALWAYS been sceptical of the notion, fostered by the nation's auditing profession, that its members were frugal types who worked in austere surroundings, setting a good example. At one o'clock, sitting in the luxurious anteroom to Signora Contrera-Kant's suite, he confirmed this view.

Signora Contrera-Kant had been one of the few women to break into commerce at the highest level; she was publicised nationally as a role model for women. Contrera was her maiden name, Kant that of the German she'd been married to. He thought about her, and tried to relax; since the decision, his tension had been inexorably on the rise. He was eager to be done with the charade of the past days.

However, he was curious to meet this woman. Not a morbid curiosity due to her infamy – a professional one. In his eyes, she was the most fascinating, the most formidable of the quartet that the ministry had required Investigating Magistrate Fabri to interview.

He'd seen sections of her dossier before it disappeared in '83 and had a good idea of how she'd climbed the slippery pole of business. He pondered, remembering facts, turning over old hypotheses.

'Be alert!' – he'd told himself the first day; he pulled himself up, and repeated it now.

But his thoughts kept running ... how had the ministry selected this particular quartet? All four were connected with the Summit Insurance Inquiry. All had been present in the city at the time of both murders. All were big names, who would invest his preordained, counterfeit report, the cover-up, with the illusion of veracity; household names, who'd provide copy which the city's captive editors could work wonders with. All were 'reliable'. Finally, in all probability, the selection had been made by the prime minister.

The fact that they were all largescale crooks, with suspected links to the mafia, was well tucked away behind the facade that the system kept propped up. Like a Wild West streetscape on a Hollywood film lot.

Be alert!

The phalanx of female secretaries flitting across the anteroom might've been cloned from those at the Provincial Bank.

One-ten, still waiting ...

Outside the armoured glass isolating the anteroom from the lift lobby, a security man prowled, harnessed with his side-arm and walkie-talkie.

The nation knew her as Signora Mail Order, although the media no longer described her thus. Several Rome editors had been persuaded not to, including one, now sacked, who'd wrongly gambled during the inquiry that the judge was on a winning streak. Twenty years ago she'd appropriated (in ways that could only be guessed at) the nationwide monopoly for the mail order business, and an empire had sprung up which put merchandise into every rural community. It must have taken immense pay-offs to maintain the monopoly. It had become folklore that when the rural citizenry looked at merchandise which fell apart before its time, they cursed Signora Mail Order. She was also principal of a major auditing group.

The financial police had nearly got their act together in '83, nearly nailed her on illegal foreign exchange out-flows. His colleague, Ruggiero, of the exchange control branch, a brilliant investigator – twice his brains – had penetrated the banking system, persuaded frightened witnesses, kept his progress under wraps. Quite a feat.

When the moment had seemed right, Ruggiero had taken his case to the attorney-general in Rome; the official had done some things which had gained the investigator's trust; anyway, it was the only way he could go forward. Then, overnight, three key witnesses had vanished, as had certain computer discs ...

Ruggiero had been a loquacious, convivial spirit. Overnight, also, he'd been transformed into a reticent, uncomfortable man; they whispered he'd become extremely well-off, though Anders had never seen signs of that, and was inclined to disbelieve it in this case.

One-fifteen ... he stirred impatiently.

Two large highly polished walnut doors sprang open, and a secretary rushed out.

He got himself out of the deep chair; his stump was burning slightly most of the time now; overuse, and the ointment gave only short-term relief.

The walnut doors closed behind him.

'Over here, Inspector.' The imperious voice, well known from her many media appearances.

He stepped onto a deep-blue, deep-piled carpet, and looked across the vast room to a group of lounge chairs distant from the desk console, and redirected his steps that way.

She sat in an armchair, that dazzling, orthodontic smile from the TV screen embracing him, measuring him, inch by inch. Powerful as a spotlight. She was smaller than he'd thought – petite. The appraising brown eyes were sardonic. For him, or for allcomers?

'Dazzling,' Anders almost murmured aloud. He was taking in the famous hairstyle: the golden swirl of a beehive, her trademark. He stood before her in his polite way. What was it about bees and power? Hadn't Napoleon adopted the bee as his personal emblem?

She was near enough to sixty, but the skin of her face and her impressive cleavage seemed alabaster-smooth. The chunky white legs, crossed, and revealed by a short skirt, looked as hard as the regional marble. And as cold, he thought. But possibly not as cold as her heart. Salvo, Rasto, and a score of others in this city had their sordid reputations, but here was an operator at a deeper and darker level, according to information which had filtered to the police over the years. Hers was an aura of dynamism, and impregnable power. It pressed at his nerves, as the others hadn't.

'Sit down, Inspector, make yourself comfortable. Is the chair satisfactory? I know of your sad disability – your sacrifice.'

He eased himself down opposite her. 'Perfectly satisfactory.' How much more did she know?

'You wish to go over my talk in July with the unfortunate Fabri?'

Anders nodded. 'Your cooperation would be appreciated by the ministry.'

'Yes? Our conversation was short. He merely asked for my views on who was responsible for the De Angelis incident. I told him what everyone here knows, a strike by a new group of anarchists. Like evil weeds they spring up, even in the best-kept gardens. But you're a national expert on that kind of infestation!'

She articulated the anarchist fiction with the winning assurance that she imposed on the TV public. Then she waited, watching him. What did she think of him? She would've been briefed on his previous interviews – including Rasto, an hour ago. She would know his checklist. They must all have their doubts about his mission – about him, by now.

He was hearing his voice repeating his tired list of questions, watching her face as she gave prompt, predictable replies. The sense of his hazard closed in.

Calm down. The desire to separate himself from these dark, flawed people rose in him. The new endeavour, paradoxically, seemed like a safe harbour to get to. If he could make it.

He abbreviated his questions, asked no follow-up ones. But plainly she wished to invest a little time in this meeting. Perhaps she fancied that she could penetrate this Rome cop's mind – and go one-up on the others. She ordered coffee, did not relent on her smile, while she poured from antique silver.

'The De Angelis inquiry caused us all unnecessary trouble. That pitiful, wrong-headed, desperate man.'

'Desperate?' He was drawn in, despite himself.

The brown eyes regarded him with simulated surprise. 'Of course. Desperate for fame, for posterity's accolade. He'd been such a failure as a judge.'

'I see.' How could brown eyes be so cold?

'*I* gave evidence for a full day – put up with his sly badgering. Was reviled in the Rome gutter-press. But in the end, of course, totally vindicated.'

He thought: Yes. The killing of the judge, and his replacement by a corrupt colleague helped with that. She'd been auditor to Summit Insurance – had assigned their fraudulent accounts, their reckless activities, a clean bill of health. No doubt when the luckless annuity-holders thought of their lost pensions they cursed her, too.

What chance did anyone have against these people? The three witnesses in the exchange control case almost certainly were dead. Ruggiero must have worked out a foolproof safety net for himself. He was smart enough.

'We in public office, must be able to stand up to criticism ...' she was saying.

He thought: You've not had to put up with much.

'... but I suffered during that period.' Her red mouth drooped sarcastically.

He recalled that the editor in the capital had been pithy: 'In her evidence, Signora Contrera-Kant has revealed herself as a liar of brilliance ...' What happened to that editor? He gazed away across the blue ocean of carpet, saw on the sunburst of a clock on the distant wall that it was 1.31 p.m. He'd carried out his assignment as mandated – all done now. He prepared himself to get out.

*

Algo had had a busy morning. The annual gathering of regional associates known in recent years as the 'board meeting' was to be held tomorrow evening. The 'chairman' had been dancing in a dark ballroom with cancer for months – that was how Algo described it to the favoured few – and he'd been carrying a double burden. Regularly he visited the clinic on a hill overlooking the city. A handful of the top bosses knew that the chairman was doomed. The question of succession would need to be dealt with soon – historically, always a potentially dangerous time. This fine room – the chairman's – had borne witness to those power plays over the decades.

The previous evening at the mayor's residence, a woman servant had been observed on the inhouse security monitors passing a message to the Rome investigator. That had been unlucky – the system was not always operative. Under questioning, she had revealed the source, the text of the message.

The investigator had met the judge's widow this morning. The news reaching Algo at 12.15 p.m. had cleared any remaining doubt from his mind. If the northern policeman's mission was as represented by the ministry, he'd have ignored the message, avoided the rendezvous like the plague; would have kept his contact with the

105

De Angelis woman to that one programmed interview.

The man's dossier was again on the desk where Napoleon's army lists had once been studied. Some of its minutiae had intrigued him. Suggestions of a double life had whispered to him. The incident which had first drawn his attention concerned a politician in Ancona who'd been instrumental in keeping a new hospital in a state of open-ended construction. Year after year, public funds had poured into the hands of a local politician and a corrupt construction group. A lawyer had threatened to blow the whistle, so the politician had murdered him and his wife. Anders had investigated, and the politician had been indicted for murder. The trial had threatened to bring the hospital scam into the open.

Despite dissuasion from his superiors, Anders, obdurately, had kept after the politician. He'd played the naive, crusading cop convincingly, and had suffered no retribution. Algo could see that he'd deceived them all. It had taken a substantial sum to pay off the judge ...

The commissioner had counselled against a bomb. This could be accommodated. A man with an artificial leg, moving about the streets, must always be in some danger. But first, he would hear what he had to say.

He glanced at his watch. This Inspector Anders would be leaving his meeting shortly.

★

At 1.22 p.m., a man called Geraci − unknown in the nation, but destined to become famous before nightfall − drove a baker's van, brightly painted with depictions of the bakery's products, out of a suburban yard, and headed towards the city centre.

He was not the van's usual driver, but a replacement. He'd driven the route the past two days to become familiar with it, and now he drove with extreme vigilance, watchful for careless drivers, mindful of traffic violations. Last month the mayor had instructed the police to increase their revenue-raising from traffic fines by fifty per cent; consequently, they'd become more creative than usual in finding offences. He trusted that he would not be stopped; however, if he was they would receive a surprise – a sawn-off shotgun was tucked down by his right leg.

Neither did he want a bump. Behind a layer of bread trays was packed 400 kilos of high-explosive, wired to detonate on impact.

He was a small, dark man in his late twenties. Like a prizefighter before a contest, he'd not shaved for two days. He was the sole survivor of his group, and its last recruit, which was possibly the reason for his survival. It was the mafia who had infiltrated the group and informed on them to the police, a fact that had filled the young man with despairing rage. The mafia had worked with the government over the years to crush leftist groups such as his. It was time that the anarchists responded in the time-honoured way. But how? A man with HIV didn't have much time. Out of the blue a man had come from Paris bringing an old, forgotten architectural drawing of the honoured society's headquarters, a plan, and the wherewithal.

The van was running smoothly. He reached the city's

heart, delicately steered around the serpentine bends of the old streets; very little traffic here.

At 1.37 p.m., he entered the dim chasm of the final street, changed down to second gear. Now he thought of nothing but his driving ... fifty metres to go to the tunnel-like gate which was never closed ...

A car's horn blared and blared, but it was locked out of the concentrated core of his being ...

★

Anders was waiting for the moment to make one of his polite departures. But Signora Contrera-Kant was still coming to the point. She smiled her brilliant smile, scanned the neutral face of this damaged, potentially dangerous policeman and said: 'Signora De Angelis deserves our sympathy. No doubt a terrible experience to have a husband taken like that. But, she is also stupid.' Her voice was now hard and level: 'Her husband made a fool of her, and now she makes a fool of herself. She's had her say. Never mind that she's wrong. Let her be satisfied. She can achieve nothing more. People should beware of her; she will only entice — seduce, I could say — others into danger in the service of a misguided cause.' Anders was silent. Was that it: a warning? 'It's possible to see how one could be lured into a deadly predicament. Don't you agree?'

He nodded slowly, acknowledging the remark. He wondered what this sardonic Signora Mail Order was like in bed. Did she dissolve into a passable imitation of a human being?

'I would very much like to show her some photographs of her beloved judge – "flagrante delicto" – with several ladies. He was very active for the past five years. There were photo-opportunities aplenty!'

She laughed abrasively, a sexual current in the air. He could see she was getting some pleasure from this. 'As though he had a fever. One might consider that this conduct disqualified him from a moral stance. We forbore from making it public during the inquiry – and then he was gone. He duped, betrayed her ...'

'Such things happen.'

'Yes. Well, Inspector, have you learned anything from our little –'

The room juddered, as though the building had shifted massively sideways, jolting their bodies and their minds. A brutal crack like thunder exploded across the city, and reverberated away, like the supersonic boom of an aircraft. Cascading down from the windows, giant shards of glass clanged on the floor.

Signora Contrera-Kant had frozen in mid-sentence, her face rigid. Their eyes connected momentarily. The phone on her console buzzed. The walnut doors sprang open and two security men rushed in, pistols in hand, and stood in the room, facing the exits. Anders twisted towards them. *Anarchist-alert procedure.*

Anders stood up.

'Inspector, I must send you on your way. Perhaps your services will be needed by the authorities.'

The sarcastic tone was still in his head when he reached the ground floor. Had she been entertaining herself with him? The cat with the mouse? He showed his card, picked up his gun from the harassed security office. Through the plateglass, still intact down here, he could see that hundreds of people had run into the street and were milling around, craning their necks towards the sky.

Behind him in the lobby, the doors of half a dozen elevators sprang open together, and dozens of bodies swarmed into the street. He went with them.

★

Signora De Angelis was two paces onto the pedestrian crossing when the explosion's shockwave smacked into her back. Grabbed by her reflexes, she whirled and dived back at the trunk of the tree on the kerb.

She heard but didn't understand the screaming traction of wheels on cobbles, the roaring of an engine, as a car flashed past in a wind-sucking black smear, skidded erratically, and speared with a vast metallic bang into the next tree along the avenue. Then she realised that it had just tried to kill her.

She had the smooth trunk of the tree beneath her gloved hands. Fellow pedestrians dotted the pavement like statues, gaping. A crazy old woman walked away, laughing knowingly, off in some other world.

A voice shrieked in her brain: 'Get off the street!' She pushed herself off the treetrunk as from a launching pad and raced over the crossing to the entrance of her apartment block.

Algo's two men scrambled out of the car staking out her apartment, parked further along the avenue. They walked over to the crashed vehicle, exhibiting wary consternation. Each had one eye on the crash and the other on the great black plume which was unfurling portentously in the sky across the city from what looked like a very specific location.

The cadaverous-faced mafioso was the first out of the wrecked vehicle. He insinuated himself through the misshapen door aperture, then leaned forward on his arms against the crumpled bonnet, head down, as though ruminating on the change of scenario. His more portly colleague struggled out the same door, a handkerchief, already bloodsoaked, held against his brow.

The men of the organisation came together. Harsh inquiries issued from the unharmed, noncommittal, monosyllabic responses from the others. The shaken pedestrians nearby came to life and scurried away.

Behind her oak door at last, shoulders against it, chest heaving, sobs retching in her throat, Signora De Angelis had woken to her nightmare. That voice was still echoing in her head. The judge's? It had been a question of centimetres, of a split-second. '*Courage!*' the voice was whispering again. '*Survival!*' it said. She threw back her head, sucked in a breath, smoothed her hair, and looked down at the broken glass from her shattered windows which littered the floor.

★

Anders paid off his taxi at a main door of a large department store. The store had a dozen such entrances, and he walked through it and came out at one where he knew there was no taxi rank. The watchers' car had been there when he'd come out of Contrera-Kant's building, but it was buried by the excited crowd, and he thought he'd escaped them. Nonetheless, he took his usual evasive action. He'd get back to his room, get off the streets until his five o'clock meeting.

Sirens sounded at all points of the compass. The taxi-drivers were voluble with rumours: 'The honoured society's headquarters is destroyed! The anarchists are back! Their leader's been sprung from the city prison in a bloodbath! Mayor Salvo, the mother-fucker, is dead! Thanks to God! ... The whole city's wired with high explosive!'

Anders let it go over his head. He'd seen it, heard it all before. Certainly, the traffic was screwed up.

Ten minutes later, exiting from the sidestreet almost opposite Bar Carella, he found a BMW parked at the door. He stared at it grimly. He was becoming a special-ist in the numberplates of mafia vehicles; but it was not one of those that had been watching over him today. He wasn't surprised that they'd found out his domicile; it had only been a matter of time.

The bar was deserted. He stood inside the door, breathing softly, listening. Similar experiences down the years did not make them easier to cope with ... There! Faint sounds of conversation from the kitchen; softly he walked across the room to that door.

Two men were in the room, their backs to him. One sat with his feet up on a large table, his hands joined, the fingers, interlaced, rhythmically flexing. The other had Cinzia pinned against the far wall, her bare arms spreadeagled against the dun, smoke-stained surface. Large hands gripped the white flesh of her upper arms, while a massive knee jammed into her pelvis seemed about to crunch it like an eggshell. He wore stylish white shoes, which appeared incongruous. He was spitting menacing questions into her face, keeping his voice down.

Anders stood silently in the doorway for a few seconds.

'Signora Carella!' he shouted.

The man at the table whipped his feet off it in one movement, then jackknifed out of the chair; the other sprang back from the bar proprietor, spun around, the big hand reaching inside his coat.

'Signora! The state of my room! I understood this establishment was well run, otherwise I would not have come here. By God! – I've been badly misinformed. Please attend to it immediately!'

Almost incoherent with anger, he roared the tirade. The two men stared at him in amazement. Their hands had frozen inside their coats. He stopped abruptly – as though the strangeness of the scene had registered with him. 'What is going on here?' he demanded suspiciously.

Breathless, looking as desirable as he remembered her at dawn this morning, Cinzia rushed around the man in her way, to his side. 'My apologies, sir! This morning … there's been a disruption … I'll attend to your room now … These are my business partners.'

He stared searchingly, disbelievingly, in turn at the three of them. 'Very well.' He turned his back on the tense silence, and left.

He went slowly upstairs, his stump hurting. His back had been crawling with tension as he'd walked out. He'd taken a big gamble. In the critical moments he'd stood in the kitchen door he'd assumed that the men weren't the colleagues of those he'd seen off in the bar, that the hands-off surveillance status continued. He'd guessed right. They'd let him go. Should he thank the anarchists – or whoever had perpetrated the bombing?

The other alternative had been to go through the door with his gun out, but Cinzia had been in the line of fire.

His room had been turned upside down as he'd assumed it would've been. His clothes were thrown on the bed, his spare leg into a corner. He walked quietly back to the head of the stairs, and listened. Cinzia's voice predominated. She had taken the cue, was upbraiding the men for the trouble they were causing her business. He nodded in admiration. Here was a woman of courage – and judgment. She knew just how far she could go with safety.

Presently, she came up the stairs, and into his bedroom.

'Cinzia, I regret this trouble,' he said. 'Are you all right?'

She tossed her head angrily. 'Pah! I'm used to these men. We are all used to them. Them, and the police.' The green eyes regarded him with an intimate interest. 'They seem to know you very well. They asked if you had visitors, made phone calls. Accused me of being in the pay of the police from the capital. Fools! I told them nothing. Nothing to tell.' She looked away, suddenly, a trace of humour on her lips. 'Nothing that need concern them.'

Anders smiled. 'Thank you.'

She began to remake his bed, the abundant flesh of her upper arms, imprinted with red marks, shaking voluptuously as she bent to the domestic task. 'No. My thanks to you, for the subtlety of your intervention. Probably, it's saved me trouble.'

He nodded.

'For you, I can't tell,' she said, lifting her handsome white face to scan him.

He smiled.

'What is this bomb?' she asked.

'Quite a large one. But how much damage it's done, to what, and from whom it's a gift, I don't know.'

He stepped forward, and put his arms around her. Their lips met in a kiss equally as delicious as their first last night. She smelt of the kitchen and cooking. All the unconstrained curves and softness of her melted against him. He thought of cheese being absorbed into hot pasta. Yes, delicious! This marvellous woman!

She watched him go from the head of the stairs. She traced her open hand down the long, thin-bridged nose, her still-moist lips. Her eyes had clouded. She thought: Where are going to now my mysterious policeman? Will you return? Will you still be alive by nightfall?

The whole city was in a ferment, and while one might ask such questions, the chances of receiving answers were about as likely as winning the mafia-run lottery.

'God go with you,' she whispered, making an investment in a lottery she still had some hope of.

Detective Matucci stood in the narrow street familiar to him from past assignments. No longer *that* familiar: its appearance was considerably changed. The debris from the three buildings to his left had come down like an avalanche, filling the street and totally blocking it to vehicles.

To his left, the front of the nondescript basaltic building was without windows; tatters of curtains and blinds flapped from the apertures. The stonework of the facade appeared undamaged. He sniffed; the powerful fumes from broken sewer pipes were mixing with the pungent odour of high-explosive.

The police inspector who had been in charge of the street-shooting locale on Monday scrambled past, eyeing Matucci accusingly, as though he should have been doing something. He said, 'This is very serious. By God! Who would have thought it?'

Matucci nodded, reflectively. A serious miss, he thought.

'Don't get your clothes dirty,' the uniformed inspector snarled, and moved on.

'Go fuck yourself,' Matucci said to his receding back.

A narrow six-storey office building of 1890s vintage had been extracted from the streetscape as neatly as a dentist whips out a rotten tooth in a mouth. It had been converted to a hill of bricks. On either side, its neighbours had had their side walls shorn off, and the office rooms where commerce had been brutally terminated at

1.37 p.m. were revealed to the world.

At the margin of the debris, a line of ambulances waited, but few had been needed. They said upwards of thirty were buried. Firemen were working in lines on the hill, putting up a show.

Lifting his head, Matucci looked again at the bare arm and hand projecting from the pile of rubble; an ambulanceman had scrambled up and found no pulse. It struck Matucci that the hand was making a fuck-you gesture to the building opposite. Poor bastard. A ricochet victim.

He'd found two witnesses. The baker's truck had come slowly, deliberately, down the street. A mafia car had sped out, horn braying, found the van in its path, swerved and sideswiped it. 'And the sky fell in!' a man had said. There'd been one man in the van. A youngish, unshaven man. Looking very tense.

There was nothing left of the van at all. Only the shrivelled, blackened chassis of the car. The bomber and the three mafia men had been blasted away over the city in millions of unidentifiable fragments.

Well, there were worse deaths.

The street was becoming darker by the minute. The shadows of hell, he thought, feeling the cold rise up to his knees. Would he ever get his life together, escape from this sewer of a city? He lit a cigarette, inhaled deeply.

'Matucci! Come here! *Matucci!*' A short, energetic individual was waving officiously to him across the wasteland. He was the chief inspector of detectives, and he'd been supervising the stringing up of tape, uselessly quartering the scene like a hound-dog. He was a man who hardly ever left his desk, and for whom Matucci had deep contempt.

A carabinieri squad car edged up the serpentine street, bouncing over rubble, for some reason its siren going. Under cover of this, Matucci pretended not to hear the summons, turned his back and ambled in the opposite direction. He would drop in at Signora Carella's bar, see if he could pick up the trail of Inspector Anders. Wasn't that his assignment?

★

Anders walked quickly across the street to the alley. The BMW was still there; its carphone was hooting. He was several paces into the alley when two car doors banged and he heard running feet. He'd previously noted a side alley on the left a few metres ahead. He turned the corner, and tried the first door. It opened and he stepped inside and closed it. He reached for a bolt, but there was none. He was in a dark hall with another door to the right. The running feet and urgent voices were directly outside. He opened the interior door quickly, and stepped into a bedroom.

The room was lit by a skylight and Anders and its single occupant stared at each other. He smiled, listening. A baby girl stood in the cot, holding its wooden sides with her chubby hands, watching him with her large dark eyes, and gave a tentative bounce. Anders kept smiling and nodding and listening.

After a few minutes, which seemed like an hour, Anders left the baby to her bouncing, quietly closed the door and stood in the hall. His face was stiff from smiling. He waited another five minutes, then cautiously opened the door and studied the alley. Empty. It was dark already – the late autumn nightfall had come as if by express. A wind had sprung up, and smacked coldly into his face. The everpresent sewer-stench did, too.

With the archway which led to Cinzia's bar at his back, he walked downhill. The rough cobbles gave him some trouble, but not too much. He veered to his left, still heading downhill, into a web of slummy streets. He heard voices, saw weak lights behind the shuttered windows of aged and decrepit housing. But only a few shadowy figures moved in and out of pools of low-powered streetlighting, their footsteps echoing in the narrow conduit.

There were too many footsteps. He stopped and edged into a doorway. He stared back up the hill into the darkness. But the wind was whining now in the street like a kicked dog, and he could make out no other sounds. He unholstered the Beretta, held it in his over-coat pocket with the 'safety' off, and went on. The few streetlights here were unlit. Ten minutes' walking down-hill would bring him out to a main avenue, then it was a short, straightforward walk to the 'safe house' on the north side of the De Angelis apartment block. He doubted if the mafia thugs would stray too far from their car; searching on foot was not their preferred method.

But he was wrong.

'Freeze!' – the command shot out of the darkness.

Anders did. From inside an adjacent house came the faint sound of radio dance music.

'Who've you got Vincenzo?' – from further away in the dark.

A beam of a flashlight hit Anders in the eyes. 'Him! The fucking cop.'

Footsteps approached: a large figure, breathing heavily, loomed at the cusp of the shaft of light. 'Well, well, the mother-fucker who's been giving us the run-around.'

He came into the light held by his colleague, and Anders saw it was the one who'd had his knee rammed against Cinzia's pelvis. His white shoes flickered in the torchlight. He held a sawn-off shotgun pointed at Anders' belly. The investigator's mind was racing. That hooting carphone had brought the change in his status he'd been fearing. Orders had come, at last, to lay hands on him.

'You put one over us in the bar, didn't you cop? Before the night's out the boss'll separate you from your nuts. In the meantime ...'

The white shoe flashed with surprising speed at Anders' groin. In a reflex action he twisted, took it on the thigh, but it sent him reeling to crash heavily on his right side. The steel works inside his left leg rattled. A pain like fire seared his stump, making him gasp.

Vincenzo laughed. 'Missed! The crippled prick was faster, Mario, you're getting old.'

The big man swore, backed away. 'Watch me this time, dickhead.'

From his prone position, Anders saw a gun-muzzle flash metres away in the darkness. The big mafioso plunged to his knees, arms flung out. The shotgun spun away, hit the cobbles and discharged with a ferocious roar so that no-one heard the next shots, which drove Vincenzo back to the opposite wall, down which he slid to pitch forward in the alley.

The torch had disappeared. No-one had come out into the street. But the radio had been turned off.

Matucci's face was above him, his service pistol in his right hand.

'What's the damage, Inspector?'

'None,' Anders said, feeling his left leg to check it was still properly in place.

Matucci extended his hand and pulled the investigator to his feet. Anders smoothed himself down, reholstered the Beretta.

'Thanks Matucci. Your timing was just right. And nice shooting.'

'I'm A grade. That was easy.'

He turned to the others. Both were dead. Big Mario remained on his knees, his torso still upright, his head bowed.

Matucci chuckled. 'Eh Inspector, looks like this piece of garbage found religion at the last gasp.'

Anders scrutinised the darkness. Listened.

'Why, Matucci? Why this ... ?'

The big detective's head was moving as he also scanned the darkness. 'Another long story, Inspector. But now we had better get away from here. You can see, the clock's speeded up. Get hold of a car, and drive north. Take secondaries. Avoid the Futuris Motorway. Especially *that* abomination. The mayor likes to see shiny new squad cars driving up and down it. But, above all, stay away from the station. Good luck.'

He gave a jaunty salute, and faded into the dark. Anders turned and continued downhill.

Five o'clock. He stood in a doorway listening to the ill-maintained, melancholic public clocks sounding the hour. One by one, like latecomers to church, the chimes pounded stonily across the river into the faces of the 1890s buildings which fronted it. His chest felt tight. It seemed like he was still trying to get his breath from the murderous encounter fifteen minutes ago. He knew it was the aftershock. He'd been there, done that. All his old 'bloodbath' days were revisiting him. What Matucci had done, he'd have to think about later.

The black plume now curled lazily for kilometres over the city, still visible even against the darkening sky. Anders watched – it reminded him of a long, paying-off pennant flown by a ship going to the breakers. If only that were the case! Well, there'd been some kind of a hit. The cold breeze ruffled his hair. He was glad of it: his clothes stank from taxi odours. Lights from the houses, the street, hovered blearily in the gloom, as though under water.

This was the hour he'd planned to quit the city. That was yesterday. Another existence. *'Like a serpent/Stealthy and sinuous steals a change/Even unto the closed heart/Seeking the reason we look/To the realm of the chaotic forces.'*

His ancestor had had his troubles too.

His stump was burning; possibly bleeding. He needed a safe place to study the evidence, write his report, negotiate the publicity. But he must wait.

Convoys of sirens still weaved through the city's distances; they seemed to never arrive at their destinations. He imagined lost souls. Three tattered drunks weaved across the road, and disappeared into the gathering darkness. Of course, it would just be pissing into the wind. All those generations, the mafia had soaked up or smothered the odd challenges which had flared briefly into the open. Officialdom had not even acknowledged its existence as a coherent force in the nation! Take Professor Roditi's book. A study of evil. It'd been skilfully discredited, and sunk into oblivion in a nationwide conspiracy involving intellectuals and politicians with mafia links ...

Well, despite Matucci's warning, he wouldn't be driving north tonight; he certainly wouldn't be on the five o'clock train for Rome. He glanced at his watch, eased the old pistol in its holster, and studied the street for a long moment. It was on a north-south axis; abruptly a stronger wind whistled by as though express from the North Pole. He turned up his coat collar.

All clear. So it seemed. He hesitated for another moment, then set out for the street which abutted the rear of the massive apartment block. At the back entrance, he pressed a bell. A few seconds passed, while he sensed scrutiny through the spyhole. The door opened on a dark interior, a shadowy woman. She ushered him in. Speechless, anonymous, she led him along an unlit passage, and let him out to an interior corridor.

These curiously resourceful amateurs, couriers of dissent. Probably a survivor of the student unrest in the seventies, when the universities were in a ferment. Some had gravitated to the leftist-terrorist groups, the Red Brigades, been discovered, destroyed, or had dropped out. Others like this, possibly more of the centre-left, had followed quieter ways of opposition to the government and the system. They had survived.

He opened a door and entered the vestibule outside the De Angelis apartment. He closed it behind him. He knocked softly on the widow's substantial oak door.

It opened instantly. He stepped into her hall, and stood beneath the weak light of an antique chandelier. She was peering at him, head on one side, as though identifying him, or not quite believing he had come. She was breathing audibly, and he smelt cigarette smoke.

'They tried to kill me! This afternoon. In the street,' — said in a long gust of breath. 'They were here in the apartment when I was out.'

She turned on her heel, and he followed her. Glass crunched under his shoes. The computer system had been assaulted: the screen was smashed, the computer itself virtually disembowelled.

She laughed bitterly. 'Ha! What fools! The people they send to do this kind of work have no brains, no education. They see nothing that's not before their noses. They've never heard of the floppy disc! Our records are safe.'

Maybe, he thought, but had they bugged the place?

'Watch what you say,' he said quietly. 'They may have placed listening devices. No names, no addresses ... Turn on your music system, radio.'

She stared at him, then went to do it.

'What happened in the street?'

124

She gathered breath, flexed her shoulders, described her experience on the pedestrian crossing, what she'd observed from the window soon after: four men had waited by the wrecked vehicle; one of them was hurt and kept a pad against his brow. Ten minutes later, two other vehicles had pulled up and six newcomers had surrounded two of the waiting men, including the one injured, and placed them in one of the cars, which had driven off. A carabinieri squad car had arrived at the accident scene, and waited a short distance away until this business had been completed. She spoke in staccato statements, rationing her breath, trying to get on top of it.

He listened, and meditated on the wreckage. An intelligence out there was functioning. Her risk status had changed; some in the mafia were now marching to a different drumbeat. And it looked like they'd been detected. He pondered this, then looked up at her stricken face.

She gestured at the wreckage. 'It has made one problem. Without a machine I can't access the information on the murders. I've made other arrangements. Come!'

He followed her to the drawing room; tonight, heavy drapes covered the window–alcove. She sat on a couch quickly crossing her long, slender legs. She was fear-stricken, but excited. Red flushes had appeared on her cheekbones; the black hair falling over her brow appeared damp. Her eyes darted at him, past him, in contrast to their morning steadiness. She lit a cigarette shakily.

He said, 'There is another problem. They've reached a decision in respect of myself – a negative decision.

Naturally, from the first they were suspicious about my assignment. I need a safe house to prepare my report. From which to contact the media. Otherwise, I should try to get out to Rome, and work from there.'

He didn't relate his day's encounters.

She sat forward and uncrossed her legs. Even as he spoke, he could not help staring at them. He observed their fine black hairs.

'From here! The other apartment you've been in tonight. That will be your safe house.'

He considered this, measured her excitement, wondered again about the realism of her expectations. Some perspective was called for. He said, 'Even if I'm successful, you should not expect too much. We both know what we're up against.'

She was peering at him through cigarette smoke. Was she nearsighted? 'Inspector, doubtless you've heard of the death by a thousand cuts?'

He nodded. These were the words of games.

She'd watched the TV newscasts on the bomb, and now gave him a terse report. It had been a car-bomb aimed at the mafia building, but had missed the target and destroyed adjacent buildings. A new group of anarchists was being blamed. Returnees from abroad. The police were on full alert. Quite like old times.

Down in the street, brakes gripped, tyres slithered. The car went on. She breathed out audibly, smiled tautly, stubbed out the cigarette. 'Come! Let's eat. I've prepared dinner.'

They ate *piccate al marsala* to the accompaniment of loud opera music. The small slices of veal, with the

126

delicious Marsala-based sauce and mushrooms would only have taken her fifteen minutes to prepare and cook, Anders knew. He guessed she could do meals like this in her sleep, come hell or high water. She'd plucked a bottle of red wine from her husband's cellar. It was old and rare, dusty and cobwebbed, a wine of national importance, a new experience for Anders. The wines he could afford seemed instantly to vanish from his palate without trace. Except last night's.

She told him that each evening of the first (and last) week of the Summit Insurance Inquiry, her husband had opened a bottle from his oldest vintages. Brooded over each bottle, as though engaged in a retrospective of the memorable wines of his lifetime.

'Each day I went in the armoured car with him to the inquiry. Returned with him each night. Heard every word of evidence spoken. Saw all the liars in action. But the facts kept slipping through their smokescreens, like darts of light. There'd been too much, too many involved to hold it all back. The dyke had sprung leaks, and it was going to collapse. On the Saturday, I wished to go with him as usual. He forbade it. I pleaded. He kissed me at the door, asked me what I'd planned for dinner ...'

The judge had had a warning, Anders realised.

He nodded slowly and asked about Detective Matucci's background. It was largely as he'd suspected. Five years before he'd been a chief inspector of detectives, but diligent work in a series of murders of small businessmen, following their defiance of the protection system, had drawn a mafia boss's ire. No convictions had been gained, but there'd been some bad publicity. Matucci had been demoted to inspector, started to drink, and then his wife had died. He'd been demoted, progressively, to detective.

She said, 'He's become a joke in the service. He's the commissioner's ex-brother-in-law. Was devoted to the crook's sister through a long illness. He's burned out – some nights he plays the drums in a jazz cellar. That's all.' Her lips articulated the last phrases with special precision. Yet again he stared, fascinated, at those small pearls of teeth.

She hadn't had the benefit of his experiences with the blond detective. It had come home to him that it suited Matucci to be regarded as a harmless comedian.

She stared across the kitchen, hands cupping her chin. 'Centimetres and a split-second,' she whispered, almost to herself. In the dim room, the gold glints in her eyes flickered, as though in tandem with her nerves.

They returned to the drawing room. The apartment was cold – no heating. 'Tonight, at eight, you'll meet ... a man. He'll brief you on my husband's murder, Fabri's – all that you need for your report.' She came up to him, put her lips against his ear: 'Professor Roditi.' His senses stirred at her scent. He tensed, raised his eyebrows. He'd been waiting for the next move, but ...

'That is dangerous,' he said.

She frowned. Was this northerner getting cold feet? Thoughtfully she lit a cigarette. 'He wishes to meet you. He has the information you'll need.'

Anders stood in the room, lips pursed, visualised the city thick with police, checkpoints. A major dragnet would be out for the terrorists. And you could bet the mafia would be on the move. He shrugged, and picked up his coat.

'I await your return,' she said.

Following her instructions, he left the apartment by the same route. A car would be waiting. He imagined her pacing through her rooms during his absence, nerves vibrating, thoughts alive with this scheme, conscious of the countermoves which would come into force ... reliving the terror of the day. Despite his intimations at the Bar Messico this morning, an age ago, he did not see her in his arms. Then he let Signora De Angelis drop from his thoughts.

From the doorstep of the northfacing apartment, he scrutinised the street's deep-shadowed doorways, saw a bug-like car do a U-turn and come back towards him.

VIII

WEDNESDAY NIGHT

ANDERS GOT INTO the rear seat of the small car. The driver, a man swaddled in a duffle coat, appeared to be youthful. Staring straight ahead he said, 'Good evening.' Then he coughed — a short bark, as though a medico had him by the balls.

It had rained, and the paving of the streets was slick with bluish light. The city felt deep into autumn, and melancholic. A bad night to be out on a mission like this. He absorbed the curfew atmosphere which the bomb had imposed on the city — though these days many avoided the night streets anyway.

They dived into a patch of sideroads and back alleys, like a fox going into a gorse thicket. Bouncing down an unlit alley they sideswiped a row of garbage cans.

'Sorry. Not the scenic route,' the driver said laconically.

They had to come out to an avenue to cross the river. In the distance, the lights of a checkpoint were aglitter. For once, all the streetlights were turned on. A few other cars scurried away in this unusual illumination. An atmosphere of fugitives on the loose was in the air. Anders felt that. Near the bridge, derelicts had dossed down in doorways. Raindrops flecked the rear window, impeding Anders' vision.

'Nothing following,' the young man said, stifling his cough.

They skidded around a corner on gleaming tram-lines, drove along the blacked-out, monumental front of the public library, slowed, and turned into the entrance. Here! Anders realised. Into this black hole they went, between the bronze statues of two famous writers of the last century. In attitudes of equal contempt, they gazed across the river at the silhouettes of darkened warehouses. Anders knew their history, and that of their sculptor, Renda, a strong man and gourmet, found drowned in the river in 1933. He'd been an excellent swimmer, but bad at politics.

A woman waited behind glass doors at the far side of a granite-paved courtyard, an insubstantial figure in a dim pool of light. These shadowy women! The car drove off as he mounted the steps.

They began a journey through corridors. Echoes of their footsteps seemed at first to go ahead, then to be behind. The woman was tense, silent, deliberately walk-ing at a moderate pace. Anders' eyes searched each intersecting corridor. They came to an ancient elevator with gleaming brass fittings – somebody's elbow grease, the last stand against the rot. In the tiny iron cage he stood face to face with the woman. Her eyes were dark in the murky confines, inches from his own, but she did not appear to see him at all. She was no longer insub-stantial, was exhaling garlic into his face.

They descended past the basement, past a sub-basement, came to a shuddering stop at a second sub-basement, jarring his stump. He swore under his breath – but more from nerves. The basements contained the stacks, kilometres of dark shelves. Few would venture here. Perhaps Anton Anders' books were buried in these millions.

Now he was inhaling dust and mildew. All around he smelt decay, felt a pressure to sneeze. Another more subtle pressure seemed to rise from the sour-smelling, moribund acres: the sense of a muttering discontent from a myriad of unread and deceased writers. The woman switched on a torch, and they entered the maze. They followed the dancing torchlight for several minutes, before he saw the light ahead. In the heart of the stacks, they came upon a small space lit by several shaded bulbs. Anders felt he was emerging into a jungle clearing.

The small man sat at a desk, sipping a steaming drink, his head with its long, yellowed hair, cocked intently. He wore the tweed overcoat he'd worn in the cathedral garden.

'My dear friend,' he said rising with energy. 'So glad you could come. So glad you are working with us.'

The ashen face, chiselled and foxy, beamed at Anders. Blue eyes sparkled with apparent humorous compassion. Why was that? Because of the intrusion into his life, the burden they were laying on him? They shook hands, he was waved to a seat, black coffee gurgled from a thermos into a cup, was handed to him. With the measured cadence of a gaoler, the woman's footsteps retreated into the surrounding wasteland.

Anders' pulse quickened; so here was Roditi's workstation. Here, in the bowels of the public library, virtually under the noses of the powers in being, a titanic work was in progress. What they'd deemed dead, or at least becalmed in the hands of the octogenarian, was alive, and forging ahead. Several tables were covered with box files and card indexes, and a camp bed was set up.

'You're very trusting to bring me here,' Anders said.

A confidential, confident smile from Roditi. 'To my rat hole? I come and go with the rats, which, incidentally, are increasing rapidly despite Mayor Salvo's budget. Even our ardent municipal ratcatchers don't venture into this subterranean paradise. That's strange, isn't it? They're the one municipal department on the bonus system.' He changed the subject abruptly. 'We've a long history of choosing the right people. Very few failures. My own life has been devoted to resurrecting past events, exposing them to analysis … making judgments … fitting them into an immense mosaic. A sense of exactitude has been allotted to me. I found your dossier interesting.'

He smiled, pouted his lips over the rim of his cup.

So Signora De Angelis had sought a second opinion. His dossier was achieving bestsellerdom.

'Unfortunately, time's short. With regard to the De Angelis and Fabri murders, the judge was a dead man from the moment he decided to be a symbol. An undistinguished life, but a distinguished death. The investigating magistrate was a weakling, but an ambitious mafia boss, whoever he may be, decided to rock the boat.'

He took up a thin sheaf of papers. 'This will give you all the sinew you require for your report. Read it now, commit it to memory. Take your time. I will fall silent, until you wish to speak.'

Anders nodded, looked out to the sea of darkness which pressed in upon their lighted island. Neither of them had mentioned the bomb. It must've shaken up a lot of ancient dust down here, given the rats a shock. He leaned over and began to read.

It was concise, almost telegraphic – names, dates, times, places; all the sinews, as Roditi said, were there, then, with scholarship, the reasons. The broad picture was as he expected. He read it again, concentrating.

They hadn't spoken of Signora De Angelis' narrow escape, though doubtless Roditi knew of it. He read on; in this stultified world, his mind seemed to be clicking away like a stove-timer. Concentrate. He lifted his head, spoke into what he felt was the dead hush of centuries.

'That's clear. Pretty much as one would expect. To be frank, the gain to your cause from my report will be shortlived, even marginal.' It was what he'd told her.

The professor had been reading something himself. He smiled warmly, waved his hand as though pushing aside a triviality. 'Our cause. You, deservedly, are a public hero. The media'll give you your moment in the sun. Where may it lead? Who knows, but assuredly, in the right direction. I admit there may be more value in your future services – if you continue to work with us.'

Anders looked at him. He had not been thinking that far ahead. 'That presumes my survival.'

'Yes, it does. You were in modest danger the moment you stepped off the train. It's no longer modest. But you're a cautious man, accustomed to danger. To coexisting with terror. We trust you'll come through.'

If Anders didn't, the professor, plainly, would accept it with equanimity.

Anders said, 'How does your work go?'

'The years '60 to '80 are done. The type's set up, the presses at secure locations, ready to go. They'll only run should I cease to exist. Otherwise, we'll choose our time. Meanwhile, I'm a thousand pages into the final volume – perhaps two-thirds done. Endlessly I sift, verify, compress, as I roam across this landscape of hell.' He grinned. 'But, of course it'll come to an end … I'll die, or I'll finish it.'

'This time – will it damage the mafia?'

'Aha! Erase the vast black shadow over our nation?' The small man in the too-large overcoat poured more coffee. 'I'll give you a little prediction. The world is what it is. Grave problems exist in all societies – social, economic, ethical. Corruption, injustice, evil, grinding poverty, great inequalities – all endemic. Everywhere, the universal darkness. The coalface, against which people like us chip away. In some societies, it's isolated to ghettoes. In our own, it's in every heartbeat, every car braking, around every corner.

'In certain countries, public opinion has freer expression, and right-minded commentators, agents for change, pour forth a river of comment – disclosing, analysing, predicting, exhorting – seeking to show the way out from the darkness. But, this myriad of words is sucked up as if by a giant vacuum cleaner. Excreted into the dustbins. Little changes. There are too many words. The messages are drowned.

'In our sad country, it's relatively fallow ground. This

time, my work will come like a thunderclap. At last, the unacknowledged, subterranean history of our unfortunate country will be written down.'

Anders stared. ' *"Like a shining sword lying in the darkness,"* ' he said, almost to himself, quoting his forebear.

The octogenarian looked at him intently, then said, 'The so-called board of the honoured society meets in this city tomorrow evening. As is customary, they will vote on important matters currently on their horizon. No doubt you will be on the agenda.

'It would be amusing, if it wasn't so deadly, how they've taken a leaf from their American brethren's book, and incorporated, so to speak.'

'Who attends?'

'The leadership. The regional bosses, their chief enforcers. About forty of the most poisonous men alive in the nation. A bunkerful of putrescent pus.' The professor smiled mirthlessly. 'Of course, they are merely the present riders in the chariot.'

He continued, 'At one remove, running behind the chariot, are the politicians, public officials whom they have in their pockets. You look at the nation's map and see regional boundaries. They mean little, deal with the superficialities of our life. The divisions of real power are not traced out on any public map. And you can take that right down to municipalities.

'As for the persons of influence, in the private sector, whom they have under their heels ... But the great mystery is – how have they kept this iron grip for so long? What drug have they administered to the nation? Why does the population sit like a hare frozen in headlights? The answers bubble to the surface in my work. Great financial leverage; an attendant web of corruption; fear, and cruel retribution; sinister secrecy, and cunning planning. Individually, the components are crude and brutal, but combined, the workings are as intricate as a Swiss watch. But, my dear, you are an expert on these matters, so I waste time.'

Anders said, 'Only when the people say "enough" will we see change.'

The professor narrowed his eyes, inspected his coffee cup. 'Yes, that is the nub of it.' He had become introspective. He murmured, 'Power. Undiluted power. That is what makes it all possible.'

Anders said, feeling a kind of release that he could talk like this, 'The nation stinks with the failure of good men, with good intentions, to come up to the work.'

'Too true, my dear Anders. Good and brave men. Chief prosecutors, investigating magistrates, police, carabinieri officers, dead in their scores. *And* their families. Rivers of blood.'

Anders, fascinated, had watched these sacrificial lambs go to their slaughter, pondered their bravery, their mentality. Chinnici, Dalla Chiesa, his old boss. And all the officers and officials before and since. Obviously, a great stride beyond his own intended action. He leaned back, out of the light. 'By the hands of human beings. Are they really such?'

'A subculture.' The professor smiled.

Anders, suddenly, without warning, was thinking in a very concentrated way. Certain questions were clicking into a queue in his mind.

'Where do they assemble?'

'At the Football Stadium, at six o'clock. In a private auditorium – a small concrete bunker.'

'Very sure of themselves.'

'My dear, they are superconfident. After decades, why not? The authorities will never touch them in this city.'

'What's the condition of the chairman?'

'Dying.'

'So it's true, Algo's running the show?'

Roditi smiled. 'Has been since his boss disappeared into the clinic. *"A man whose brain is a maze of cold corridors, along which proceed lethal thoughts."* ... A sentence from my work. And now – someone is trying to knife Algo in the back.' He'd not ceased smiling.

'The terrorists?'

'Well – until today, I confess I believed them extinct. It may have been a last throw. But what a throw! Unfortunately a near miss.'

Anders was both listening, and thinking along the new line. All quiet. He'd a notion that phrases, sentences, other than the professor's, were in sibilant dark flight all around them like arrows. The pressure of time sliding by brought him back to the illuminated island, the professor's expectant face.

'Signora De Angelis is in grave danger.'

'Yes ... today's incident. That was against the grain. I fear she's at risk from a renegade faction. Ambition is in play. I surmise it's the group that killed the investigating magistrate and your undercover man. Despite the odds, she's managed to project her face, her story, to the nation. It's saved her so far. She's anti-mafia, anti-establishment to the core — a very personal vendetta since the judge's death. Your report, your actions, might help her. I do hope so. I've no doubt Algo will be working hard to run this faction to ground. God help them when he does! Of course, they may get him first.'

Anders said, 'Well, I should begin my work.'

Roditi reached into a drawer, produced a thick packet of money. 'Use this as necessary.'

The woman had returned and was waiting outside the patch of light. Anders got up and leaned forward to shake the hand which the professor presented to him with a flourish. The writer's spectacles glinted in the light. He exuded pleasure. 'Go safely!' He became still, his head held like an animal testing the wind. He said, 'Anton Anders, 1872, *The Night Serpent*. A mysterious man. Not a great poet — but, certainly, undervalued.'

The northern policeman stared at him. He'd never met another person who knew of his forebear. The professor had spoken as though there was no discontinuity between Anders' earlier muttered quotation and his own comment. He felt he'd been given an insight — as sharp as a camera flashlight — into the workings of the octogenarian's fabulously-stocked mind. A vain man, lover of actresses in the '30s and '40s, of young men all his life.

It was ten o'clock. The small car had returned. They drove under the arch, into the riverside avenue. The lights here had been switched off. The professor, obviously, was a man who turned switches on in people. He was as coldblooded in his own way as any mafia boss, as selfish a manipulator of human beings. But, of course, for different ends ... Suddenly, an image of the two dead mafia thugs killed by Matucci five hours ago was in the forefront of his mind; but he dismissed it as quickly, said to the anonymous driver, 'Is there a place open near the apartment where I can make a phone call, get coffee?'

Such places always existed around corners, down stairways. They drew up outside a small cafe, where transvestite prostitutes waited under a bleary streetlight. Anders wished the driver goodnight; the car turned a corner, quit his world. The echo of a cough remained in the freezing street.

★

It had been a day to remember — even in Algo's extensive and variegated experience. He'd been at his desk when, in one cataclysmic instant, the earth-shaking shock from the building's basaltic bowels struck his body, his senses, and the room's four large windows had imploded. For a mini-second, he'd been in peril. The air had whined with flying glass. A ferocious bone-shaking 'kerthump' had sundered the neighbourhood's customary sullen silence — as though a hellish battery of massive pile-drivers had simultaneously pounded into a building site.

He'd sat rigidly in his place as the sounds of falling debris were imposed on the eerily reinstated silence, a glass shard hanging from his cheek, another from the shoulder of his suit. The room had filled with agitated aides, and he'd remained motionless, his usual dead-pale face as set as stone, asking himself: How can this be? And who?

The anger had come later, after a briefing on the known facts of the outrage; the chief of security had endured a scarifying thirty minutes. Then a report on the attempt to run down the De Angelis woman had reached him, and his anger had increased to a white-heat.

Algo said to the security chief: 'What have you done with those two?'

'We're holding them downstairs.'

'Have they talked?'

'There's not been time.'

Algo smiled coldly. 'Of course. Put them into the white room, and let them ponder their futures.'

'I will attend to it personally.'

'Yes, that would be a good idea,' Algo said, his voice hard and level. 'I *do* want the name, or names, of those behind them.'

Alone, he continued to sit at the famous desk, staring across the room towards the perhaps no longer priceless medieval tapestry, now impregnated with a hurricane of glass splinters, which glinted festively in the electric light, running on an emergency generator.

He thought: As hard to eradicate as cancer cells. He was not reflecting on the tapestry; he had the anarchists in mind. He narrowed his eyes, and examined the chess board with its intricately-carved ebony pieces, set out in a problem. Usually, he slept only four hours, and in the small hours relaxed with chess and other problems.

Tomorrow night he was going to turn up the heat on

the organisation's elite. He would hit them with the force of today's bomb. Blast them out of their complacency, and their disloyal intrigues. Concentrate their minds on the main-game. *Affirm* his succession to the leadership.

A manservant brought him cognac, and he sipped it meditatively. Complacency, overconfidence, inefficiency had infiltrated their affairs. Major errors had occurred. An odour of staleness permeated the organisation; revenues were down substantially.

And, the canker of treachery was somewhere in their highest ranks. The first clear signal of it had come with the assassination of the investigating magistrate; then the murder of the undercover cop; today's renegade actions had the same distinctive imprint. Such crises had occurred down the years, had been dealt with by the leader of the day, or he'd ceased to be leader, and had finished up in the States, or South America – or on a slab. Algo smiled at history. He had no doubts as to his own place. He would deal with it.

Questions like Professor Roditi needed revisiting. Had that old man really drifted into a twilight of senility as the reports claimed? Recently, on an impulse, he'd re-read the dangerous book which had come out in the late sixties. They would bring him in. Care would need to be taken; the detention or death of the octogenarian might be a trigger for the release of another dangerous work. To be avoided at all costs! The ever-reliable commissioner should attend to it; by sleight of hand he could be passed from the police into their care. He would enjoy milking that antique mind dry. Bone-dry.

This Anders – could he be connected with the so-called anarchist bomb? Had that been the real agenda? What a fascinating proposition! Or, in the vernacular of their American colleagues, was something still to come from left-field? His mind continued roving a dark landscape, drafting the restructure, which would be painful for many, fatal for some.

★

Anders pushed his way past the whores into the cafe. A few people from the neighbourhood sat at the bar, at tables, drinking wine and coffee; their heads turned, but they avoided eye-contact. He took a corner table and a chair facing the door, ordered coffee.

The coffee came, and he forgot it. He stared at a whitewashed wall. It disappeared from his consciousness, and he was gazing at a materialising picture. A blueprint. He was totally absorbed ... it'd be a blinding reversal of play in his life.

He thought on, now doubting its feasibility.

In all probability it would be the end for him. He couldn't see a way around that. Coldly, he meditated on this. Not on his life but on his abandonment of the poet, on the sacrifice of that reserved time he'd been obdurately working towards. He could feel it slipping away from him, like a winter sunset.

But there'd never be another opportunity like this. Never again such a chance to reverse the direction of the nation's life. To strike a major blow. To do real damage. If it could be done.

By a confluence of events, he'd been brought to a lighted window, was staring in at a room which was the future defined.

He felt this intensely.

The deeper dimension came out of the night like an arrow. These past days, the poet's voice had been in his head as never before. Something had been building up. Going on. Falling into place. Through time and space, a wheel had been turning, and tomorrow, its shadow would fall over this city.

Abruptly, the circumstances of the death of Anton Anders were on the white wall, in his mind, and he was marvelling at it all. Anton Anders had been killed in a duel in January 1875; on the eve of commencing his masterpiece. He had been convinced that it would be a great work, and his notes showed that in ambition it far outshone *Night Serpent*. A landholding neighbour had grievously ravished the poet's housemaid. It was the most recent of brutal attacks that the man had perpetrated on serving women of the district. The man appeared above the law. Anton Anders had demanded satisfaction. His neighbour, an ex-cavalry officer, was a notable duellist. Pistols were chosen …

The investigator continued to stare ahead as this history rolled through his head. The images were as sharp as though he'd been present.

What were the poet's thoughts on the eve of the duel which, logically, could have only one result – unless something remarkable occurred? Despair for his unfinished work? Regret for his unfinished life? Worry for his dependants? Friends pleaded with him to withdraw. He resisted all pleas, even when they were on the field. Much of his poetry had been about justice, and courage in the face of oppression.

Anders imagined him steeling his will.

Anton Anders took a bullet precisely between the eyes. A month latter, the neighbour had been brought to trial, subsequently executed. To rape and terrorise the peasants was one thing; to kill a fellow landowner, another.

Anders was suddenly convinced that his ancestor had made his sacrifice consciously, achieved his aim. Although perhaps he'd hoped against hope to have the good fortune to outshoot the cavalryman; nothing was absolutely certain in such affairs.

The cold of the night sifted down the steps into the basement cafe, overwhelmed the feeble heating. So the poet would remain obscure. Anders gazed at the wall, like someone who has, at last, accepted that a love affair is dead.

He picked up the cup, had a mouthful of lukewarm coffee. He was perspiring. His face cleared. His body became relaxed. He was seeing the slogan painted on the wall: *'A day without wine, is a day without sun.'* He got up, and went to the phone.

He referred to the card, and dialled the number. The receiver lifted. 'Hullo, Matucci.'

'Matucci,' he said, 'it's Anders.'

'You're still here, eh!' the detective's surprised exclamation made Anders' ear ring.

'Still here, still alive. The line?'

'Clear this end.'

'Can you meet me – right now?'

Matucci would come in twenty minutes.

Anders was taking a risk on the detective's phone being untapped. Given his present-day status in the force, they probably didn't worry about him, and he seemed confident.

Tonight's affray in the street had enabled him to make up his mind about Matucci, in one dimension anyway. He knew which side of the fence the local detective was on. Unlike himself, Matucci had never been sitting on it; with his convoluted persona, he'd just been keeping the enemy confused.

He returned to his table, ordered fresh coffee. This time he was tasting it. Some things still worked down here. Even in this lousy bar, the coffee was well made.

Matucci was quick. He entered, at this hour as jaunty as ever, looking suave in a stylish trenchcoat. But he took a thorough detective's look at the establishment as he pulled out a chair opposite Anders.

'I thought you'd have got out,' he said reprovingly. 'Be headed back to the bosom of the ministry.'

'There's been a change of plan,' Anders said. 'And I need your assistance.' He looked at the detective's strong, broken nose, the slimline moustache, the longish blond hair. He was remembering his remarks in Cinzia's bar, seeing him standing over the bodies of the two thugs, pistol in hand.

He checked they couldn't be overheard, and said seriously, confidentially, 'I need what is on this list by tomorrow noon.' He put the page from his notebook into the detective's hand.

Matucci's eyes widened as he read the carefully printed specifications; slowly, he sat back in his chair. He stared at Anders with a new, calculating expression. 'Christ!' he said, softly but emphatically.

He was not referring to the request; he was acknowledging the amazing decision which clearly lay behind it. He shook his head. 'Eh–eh–eh! Inspector, life is full of surprises.' He brought out his cigarettes, methodically lit one. 'Especially after today.'

Anders nodded. 'Can you do it? Will you do it?'

The detective had ordered a drink, and now he drank half of it off at a gulp, glass in one hand, cigarette in the other. He put down the glass, patted his lips, and stared at the tabletop with narrowed eyes.

'Yes,' he said, 'I will do it. It's not easy to get hold of what you want – in this city. But I'll call in some favours. Some ordinary crims in this city are my best friends. For instance, there's a safebreaker. I'll get it.'

Anders relaxed, imperceptibly. 'Use a courier service, and have it delivered by noon to … here.' He tore another page out of his notebook, wrote down the address of the safe house. 'Memorise this, destroy it.'

He leaned back, raised his cup to his lips, watched the detective burn the paper in the ashtray.

'Today's excitement?'

Matucci, quietly for him, described the scene of the explosion, gave the facts so far as they were known. He said, 'A witness saw the bomber at the last moment – a solemn young man he said, looking very tense.'

'Understandable,' Anders murmured.

Matucci nodded, surveyed the room. 'It's a great pity

it wasn't more productive. Anything else, Inspector?'

Anders shook his head, his business completed. It was best if Matucci knew nothing more; besides, he was still working on it in his head. The euphoria had gone. Now he felt very still within himself, quietly committed. There was one other thing. He took out the thick packet which Professor Roditi had given him. 'With luck, what's in here will cover you.' The detective pocketed it without a word. He winked. 'Maybe there'll be something over to go on the town.'

Anders pondered, remembered something: 'Are you playing jazz these days?'

Matucci gave him a quick look. 'Yeah. I'm a drummer.' Briefly, he played bongo drums on the table. 'This city is perfect for the blues. Though, maybe it's gone a long way beyond that.'

Anders raised his cup: 'To better days.'

'Whatever the undertaking, good luck,' the detective said. He knew what big event was to take place in the city tomorrow evening. He was still trying to get his mind around the incredible notion.

'Many thanks for your help.'

They shook hands. Musingly, Matucci stared at the northern policeman's left leg. He raised his eyebrows, shrugged, grinned, and left, rolling his body adroitly between the tables.

Presently, Anders followed him into the deserted street. The whores had disappeared. The old buildings stood shuttered, stonefaced, scoured of life, time-compressed, impervious to human hopes and suffering – yet redolent of them.

Suddenly, he remembered: '*In my ancient town / The night's black, dense paragraphs / Punctuated by commas of errant light / Tell nothing more than is needed.*' That had been written of another town. The hillside town where the poet had been born and bred. Once, on leave, Anders had gone there to do his research. Just two weeks. He thought of it as the happiest time in his life.

The shade of Anton Anders had moved in closer. Would his ancestor be on the welcoming committee? With a grimace, he tossed the thought away. His mind shifted to the more immediate welcoming committee likely to be awaiting his return to the Bar Carella. And return he must. He needed his spare leg; he regretted not having taken his suitcase this morning. For the fourth time that day, he eased the Beretta in its holster.

He came along the alley slowly, and quietly. He'd taken a wide detour around the streets where the two mafia thugs had been killed. There were no signs of police activity in the area. At their idiosyncratic intervals, he heard sundry clocks strike midnight. These alleys were deserted wind-tunnels, littered with uncollected garbage. Ahead, where the alley debouched under its archway into Cinzia's street, he made out the black mass of an obstruction. For a moment he stared. Then he had it: the rear half of a parked car, projecting across the opening.

The bar was less than twenty metres downhill to his right on the other side of the street. Silently, he walked back down the alley to the next street.

A lone telephone booth stood on the corner. He

entered it and dialled the emergency fire department number, spoke authoritatively. Then he returned, passing the door behind which, presumably, the baby girl slept, retrieving the newspaper he'd noted in a trash basket. Rats went twittering down the alley in Indian file. The ripe stink of rotting debris came on the wind. He crept through the archway to the car's rear. Phew, the damned sewers ... Thirty metres downhill a solitary light burned above Cinzia's door: for him?

It was difficult to kneel, but he got down by degrees. He was hard against the rear section of the long car, kneeling in the darkness under the archway. 'Let us pray,' he intoned silently. He sighed with relief: no lock. With gentle pressure he turned the cap to the fuel tank, felt the airlock snap. Little by little, he unscrewed the cap; it was free in his fingers. Carefully, he placed it on the ground.

Down in the city, sirens had started up. The signature tune of the day, he thought grimly. The mafioso in the front seat coughed, shifted his position. Sloppy. He should have been waiting in an ambush down the alley. Superconfident, the professor had said.

Deftly, he fed the long paper spill into the tank, withdrew it, tasted petrol, reinserted it. It was always a help to have done things before. Now he needed great care — and luck. The metal lighter for ladies' cigarettes was cold in the palm of his hand. The end of the spill fed back into the alley. He hunched his body over it, cupped a hand around it, flicked the lighter. He held his breath. The flare of light seemed extreme, was gone. The spill was burning confidently.

Cautiously, he stood up, fatalistically accepting the

151

creaking of his leg. Precisely, he edged around the stone buttress of the arch, keeping flat against the wall.

A memory ... *He'd been stuck fast in his bombed and burning car, fixed upright in the wreckage, streaming liquids. His brain, blown out of his body, had floated in the sky with the black smoke. Pain had advanced on him in red waves, his world was ablaze. But two passing plumbers had got him out ... men with strong wrists, and burred fingers used to stubborn metal ... Safely out, he'd begun to scream ...*

His heartbeats surged. The scream in his head had turned to a scream at the bottom of the hill: sirens had converged there.

WHOOMPH! A furnace door flung open – red flame gashed the darkness. The searing wind went past Anders' face. The blast of heavy air jolted the buildings. The guttural whoompf of the petrol tank had slugged the night silence. In an intense, orchestrated vibration, glass in a hundred windows whined, then tinkled down on stone with a ridiculous delicacy.

Two men ran vigorously from the bar. They sagged at the knees, staggered momentarily, as the heat hit them, then came on at the car, the rear half of which was now blazing mightily. Windows, doors were banging, abruptly vocal people in nightclothes came spilling from houses. Enforcing its own pulsating, light-flashing pandemonium, the fire brigade arrived.

Anders stepped out from his doorway, walked quickly through the shocked, night-attired residents. Heat beat back from the walls. A surviving window exploded like a gunshot, sending people ducking. He slipped into the bar, climbed the stairs, was in his room. The work of seconds. His suitcase was on the bed. He flipped open the lid. It was packed, the spare leg on top. In one movement he shut the lid and swung it off the bed, went out the door.

At the end of the passage, Cinzia appeared in her doorway, a glowing vision in a white nightgown. Frozen in mid-stride he made out the long, thin bridge of her nose, the low-slung hills of breasts. Spontaneously, he held up a hand in salute. They kissed gently. Then he was going down the stairs.

The car was aflame and roaring from end to end. At a safe distance, a hundred or so people milled around. He inserted himself into the crowd. Torrents of foam whooshed at the fire from several directions. Down the street, rapid blinking lights turned the buildings blue. Between fire-streaked figures he glimpsed a large man sitting on the cobbles, head supported by a pair of big hands, coughing his lungs out.

Then he was away from it, walking steadily downhill, heading for more complicated work.

IX

THURSDAY MORNING

FOR THE SECOND TIME in the past hours, Anders entered the northside apartment, using a key given him by Carla De Angelis. She had asked him to call her by her first name. He stood in the dark listening, suitcase in hand; his rate of breathing seemed to match the city's flickering nightpulse. He imagined he could hear his heartbeats. He fumbled for a switch, turned on a feeble hall light, looked at the substantial, wine-red curtains which covered the northfacing windows, and several large tapestries draped on other walls.

Ten minutes later, in the dining room drinking coffee, he began the search for the ignition point of his plan. He needed his brain to be as clear as it had ever been. All the day's incidents and tension were blocked out by his professional training.

She was incapable of a quiet approach; her heels came clacking along the corridor he'd traversed earlier. He'd been expecting her. He glanced at his watch: ten minutes past two. She entered the room as active, as wide awake, as she'd been an age ago, in the Bar Messico. Her eyes darted to his suitcase, flashed back to his face.

'Ha! Did all go well?'

He nodded. 'Yes.'

Without another word she went to the kitchen. He heard her opening cupboards. An oldfashioned typewriter, a sheaf of paper, waited on the dining room table. He wouldn't be using them now, although she didn't know that.

Over soup and fresh bread, he described his meeting with the professor. It was now irrelevant, but she expected a report. He did not mention the incident in Cinzia's street. She listened in silence, watching his face, bringing her probing intensity to bear on him. He watched doubt float in and out of her eyes. This was a woman who lived on her instincts as much as anything. Had she sensed the new dimension of determination in him?

It was four hours since he'd left her to go to the meeting with Roditi, but her mood, her nervous state hadn't changed. He watched her walking in the room, distractedly smoking her cigarette, tossing her hair back from her brow with sharp head movements, her eyes shifting here and there, her dark face dense with the thoughts she was marshalling. He seemed to hear her nerves crackling in the air.

It was a brave performance, and he wished there was something he could do to help her quieten down. Two days since he'd first set eyes on her – since the fascination had begun its weaving, chancy run. She turned to him and he felt her willing him to the typewriter, to the report.

But she had to talk – to get thoughts out of her head.

The brown-gold eyes held his, entreating his whole-hearted conversion: 'Professor Roditi is an individual without passion. This is what's saved him, kept him going all the years like a marathon runner.' Her lips sculpted each word, fighting the throatiness. 'A spent force, they think! Ran his last race, long ago. Ha! He's like a limpet, fastening onto the myriad information which he's dredged up. With all his experience of knowing where to search. Fitting it into that long, desperate story. He's a great man.'

Anders watched her, kept his counsel. Arms crossed under her breasts, she stared back at him, said quietly, in a change of tone, 'God forbid that they wake up to him. That's one data bank which can be smashed.'

'That is the problem. Have you read the book which is finished?'

She had another cigarette aglow, smoke around her head. 'Of course.' Suddenly, weariness overpowered her. She leaned against a wall, eyes downcast, the hand with the cigarette dropped to her side, the ash falling away. This tempestuous day, at last, was applying the screws. She looked very desirable.

He nodded slowly and went out to the kitchen. He needed a quiet moment to think, settle himself down, find a glass of brandy. Despite everything, the other had entered his head.

Making love to her had been on his mind from the first; in its separate compartment. He'd recognised the kind of atmosphere which made it a possibility. There had been an offer in her eyes in the Bar Messico, and he understood that she was a woman who kept her promises.

He pondered: was it an unfair move in her present state of mind? But everyone was fearful. All his women had had some part of their lives trashed. He knew it would be tonight or never. He turned to her as she entered the kitchen. Three paces apart they looked at each other curiously, penetratingly. At that moment, he thought she was the most beautiful woman he'd ever seen. 'Carla,' he said.

He helped her fold back the weighty damask bedspread on the huge wooden bed with its handcarved decoration: her woman friend, also a widow she'd said, must be lonely in it. Beyond the apartment's walls, the city's pulse, shallow and flickering earlier, had diminished to the quietude of a hibernating animal's.

The cold touched her lips like a frozen hand; she visualised mist curling over the surface of the river, disconnecting the bridges from terra firma. She watched him remove the artificial leg.

Anders surrendered to the moment – as always on these occasions. Nothing in his life held more meaning. Once again he was connecting with another human being, with their unique experiences, labyrinthine memories; a persona with tensile nerves, raw courage ... a tortured soul. It was a harvest for his sympathetic and perceptive nature. His lips pressed against her mouth, his tongue traced over the teeth, he sucked in gusts of her breath. It was like living through a day of quicksilver weather: shadows and shine, sharp showers, outroaring of wind, sprints and lulls. His hands found the rich, abundant flesh with which the years had endowed her hips. He had a notion come and gone in a flash that it was like the clean, pale silt in the long curves of a river's flood plain. But still, a slim woman ...

His mind swooped in helicopter-mode along the declivities of ferny valleys above secret, reedy streams – a fantasy multiplying from a fantasy.

It ended, in an amalgam of wet, too-warm flesh, tangled sheets, and hard-breathing sleep.

Awake in the early hours, he remembered her crying out: 'It's been five years!' The judge had been dead for just over one. Not a mystery: in his last years he had had mistresses, Anders knew from his dossier, hadn't needed Contrera-Kant to tell him.

He'd remained the light of her life. She'd never wavered – or so it seemed; *there* was the mystery.

What a day. He thought of wide-shouldered men in thick overcoats brooding in a car on the south side of the building; then of other mafia vehicles hissing down wet streets paying calls here and there, waking up terrified citizens.

He thought of their lovemaking: *not* a reward, but a precious gift. Then sleep claimed him.

★

The commissioner woke to the buzzing of his phone. Shit! The clock on his bedside table showed three. He allowed himself a couple of seconds to clear his mind of his dream and took up the receiver. He'd been at headquarters until 2.00 a.m., coordinating with various national agencies the dragnet for the anarchists, or whoever the fuck was responsible.

Into his ear, his brain, came Algo's voice. 'My regrets for the disturbance. What news on the perpetrators of the outrage?'

'None yet. A large force is deployed.'

'Very well … I need your cooperation.'

The commissioner sat up, his wife slept on. Both were accustomed to this kind of call. 'What can I do?' he replied quietly.

'After midday, I gave instructions for our northern visitor to be brought in. However, he's avoided our people. Tonight, he caused some trouble.' He sketched what had occurred outside the Bar Carella. 'Earlier, two of our people were killed in a nearby street.'

After a long pause he said, 'He is working to an altern-ative agenda – his own, or one sponsored by our opponents in the capital. Either that, or he's gone mad, which I consider unlikely. Yesterday morning he met the De Angelis woman again. It's all of a piece.'

The commissioner listened, stroked his stubbled cheeks. This inspector was a rare one. He felt a rising pressure.

Algo said after a brief silence, 'I suspect he's found a safe house. But he's a man on a mission, and will come out.'

'What can he be up to? Is he planning to write a report of some originality, do you think?'

'Perhaps. The point of my call is your man Matucci. A few hours ago he acquired explosives. Unfortunately for him, he gambled without luck on the sanctity of an old friendship, an old favour.'

The commissioner felt the pain begin to uncoil once again in his stomach.

'Now, what is he up to, with this extraordinary action? He's your watcher on this Rome cop, I'm informed. Your judgment on that point could be questioned, could it not? At any rate, what is the true nature of their relation? I think Matucci should explain himself. It's possible he knows where our visitor is presently lodged, what his intentions are.'

The commissioner rubbed his stomach gently, cursed inwardly. What was coming next?

'I'm going to have him picked up for a little chat. My dear commissioner, I'm aware of your family relationship, so if he cooperates, we'll go softly. Otherwise ... '

The commissioner replaced the phone receiver gently, groaned quietly, and lay on his elbow in the dark. Could this troublesome investigator be connected to the massive bomb? The question, not articulated, had been in the air during the call. And what, in God's name, was Matucci up to? He sighed bitterly to himself. Algo had been suave as usual, but the weight of the matters on his mind, and his deadly intentions, were clear.

He'd kept his voice low, and his wife had not stirred. Sleep on, he thought morosely, in your untroubled life of fluttering around the elite boutiques, the glossy restaurants, the elegant bridge parties, while your husband worries and rots in his guts. He felt a deep uneasiness – a sense of events in motion which had bypassed him.

The phone rang again. Shit! He picked up the receiver.

'It's me, your one and only.' The mordant-humoured voice of Signora Contrera-Kant came into his ear. Dear Christ! this was too much. Of all his mistresses, only this one would ring him when he was in bed with his wife. He cupped his hand over the receiver.

'Yes?' he said.

'What news on the anarchist bastards?'

'None. A dragnet is set up. I was at headquarters till two.'

'Keep me posted. Are you going to fuck me on Saturday afternoon?'

The commissioner, squeezing the receiver against his ear, said that was his intention, the emergency permitting. She rang off with the laugh that irritated him beyond words.

His wife turned over in one movement, wide awake. 'Who was that?' she asked. He stared at her dark form in surprise. 'They treat you as a servant,' she said in a matter-of-fact tone, and rolled back to sleep.

Yes, that's quite correct, he thought. But it's what I am, and why I'm where I am. And, it's been exactly the same with the long line of my predecessors. He lit a cigarette, and smoked in the dark. His wife hated him smoking in bed, but tonight he deserved a special dispensation.

★

'In the first week of Spring, 1922, the leadership of the honoured society held its annual meeting at the football stadium,' Professor Roditi wrote in his careful script, between

2.00 and 3.00 a.m., Anders' visit last night a remote event in his mind.

'Giacomo Valenti presided. *Fifty-two members were present, and the usual security men. An extraordinary item of business was on the agenda. It related to PS Bossi, a bar owner in the city of Perugia; this unfortunate man had been troublesome to the collectors for some time; the usual measures had been taken against him (his bar had been wrecked, and himself severely beaten in separate incidents), but he had proven obdurate, even to the extent of prevailing upon several other bar owners to join his resistance to the protection racket. It had been decided to make a special example of him.*

'During this period, the usual method of correction was execution by shooting: two bullets in the head, and the corpse left in a back alley. However, a more elaborate fate had been prepared for poor Bossi.

'At nine o'clock on that May evening, before the assembled top bosses, he was strapped naked to a meat-packer's preparation bench, and a pork butcher, Santucci, long in the organisation's pay, slaughtered and butchered him according to the methods of his trade. A source claimed that the man's remains were later processed through an industrial mincer and sent out as pig-food.

'Even to this assemblage it must have been a memorable experience. Much later, one member, Gianluigi Valesio, (see p. 333), is on record that there was a general condemnation of this act. No doubt, the suits in the front rows had been liberally sprayed with gore and ruined; and explanations at their homes when they returned might have been unpleasant in some cases.

'The unfortunate Bossi took several minutes to die under

the pork-butcher's ministrations, and doubtless his screams reverberated unpleasantly in that concrete bunker of an auditorium. Interestingly, the organisation had once before used this salutary method of correction – in 1921, with the town clerk of Pisa – who had attempted to bring to the notice of the authorities, in the capital, a monstrous fraudulent transaction involving the sale of public lands, (see Rigor Mortis, p. 977).

'After the Bossi affair, all was quiet among the bar owners in the nation ...'

Roditi laid down his pen, gently, precisely – almost in a valedictory gesture. He glanced at the fan of index cards spread before him, then brought his hands under his chin.

After midnight, a message had come to him via the woman who walked through the stacks-maze like a gaoler. Disturbing though long-expected intelligence from police headquarters, apparently from that complex individual Matucci: 'Stay away from your flat, keep out of sight,' it said.

Matucci? Well, why not? When a clown took his makeup off, who did you see? Today, tonight, much had happened – was in the air. Now they were looking for him. Of course, he'd been left in peace all these years because they hadn't any longer seen him as a threat; that was one of the changes in the air. He stared into the darkness beyond his lighted enclave. An unpalatable thought had come: Had the impressive Inspector Anders sold him out? ... In this world, who could tell?

He looked down at his desk. He'd sent the signal, held in abeyance for years, and in two remote towns printers had hurried through the darkness to their workplaces. By now, *Rigor Mortis II* would be rolling off the presses.

At some distance, there was a twittering sound as the rats went about their business in the stacks. The professor grinned happily: the explosion seemed to have energised them. They never worried him. He found them amusing companions, felt they were on his side – certainly against that murderous crook, Mayor Salvo.

★

This was the day he was going to die. Unless something amazing happened. It was Anders' first thought when he woke. Not a thought to trifle with. But neither was it one to be overwhelmed by, given the life that he'd led. It had always been waiting around corners – just like his women. The difference was that the consummation had been postponed. Nonetheless, it was a thoughtful moment.

Carla had gone – not long ago. A cup of coffee steamed beside him on a table. He heard traffic faintly in the street, a strange, everyday sound, after a night of such incandescent character.

His breakfast was set in the kitchen. He ate it, and then showered and shaved in a big, oldfashioned bathroom. As usual, while he shaved, he thought of odd, irrelevant matters.

'She hits the high notes nicely,' his friend Arduini had said of the mature understudy to the principal soprano of the National Opera, whom Anders was having an affair with. The colonel and Anders had adjoining flats, a common wall. The soprano had had an astonishing sexual fantasy about his stump ...

Water gurgled in the aged pipes of the heating system: its rheumatism. He'd not touched the curtains, and it was necessary to put on electric lights. He finished his ablutions, sat in an armchair, and began to go over in his mind the bomb-building techniques he'd learned in his days on the anti-terrorist squad.

★

At a vast distance, Detective Matucci's phone was ringing. His mind came swimming up out of deep sleep. He fumbled for the receiver, he'd slept only four hours.

'Darling!' Paola's breathy voice gusted into his ear. 'He's left for headquarters. The damn phone kept ringing all night. Can we meet Saturday afternoon – Antonella's flat, this time?'

Matucci sat up, glanced at his watch. Six-thirty. 'Sure. I think I'm off duty. But it might change.'

'Try to make it, darling. I can't wait! Can we do it our special way? Missing you. Ciao, darling.'

Matucci stood under the shower, his fair hair flattened against his handsome head, smiling slightly. The 'special' way – he hadn't realised there was one. The commissioner's wife was a wildcat in bed; after their Saturdays, he had scratches all over his chest. The commissioner, apparently, had relegated her from his gallery of pleasures. Paola had been kind to him after the death of his wife, her sister-in-law.

The phone rang again. It was him.

'Matucci! You're in dead trouble! What've you been up to you stupid bastard?'

'Up to, Commissioner?'

'Don't tell me! I don't want to know. Listen, get out of town. Now! That's if you want to keep your miserable life.' The commissioner sounded extremely agitated.

'Eh! Commissioner, will I be on full pay?'

'Christ almighty!' the commissioner snarled, and crashed down the receiver.

Matucci towelled himself off quickly, had a fast shave, dressed with his usual care, strapped on his pistol. Early this morning, on his return to his flat, he'd meticulously cleaned the weapon, reloaded the three spent shells. He picked up the small overnight bag, always packed against contingencies – that was the thoughtful Matucci the world didn't see – and from a table took the carton wrapped in thick brown paper.

From just inside his building's lobby, his ice-blue eyes comprehensively searched the street: no suspicious-looking vehicles, no loiterers. The usual early morning commerce in play. Fog blurring the distance. Even this early, the stink of petrol fumes. Nothing. Even so, he was trusting fate as he stepped smartly down to the pavement. The carton under his left arm was heavy, but Matucci was big and strong.

He walked three hundred metres to the courier office, again scrutinised the street, and entered. At a bench, he wrote on the carton the alias Inspector Anders had provided, and the address, gave a false name and address for the sender. He handed it to a clerk, instructed it was to be delivered before noon, paid, and left.

For a moment, he considered whether to risk his car. What the hell! However, he stood for a good few minutes behind his apartment building scrutinising the narrow street, his garage door. Only his portly neighbour was in view. The man shut his own garage door and drove off to his men's outfitting shop. Matucci knew the occupations of all his neighbours, and especially this one.

'Okay,' the detective breathed. He crossed to his door, unlocked it, raised it, and stepped inside the garage. Something hard and metallic hit him in the middle of the spine.

'Don't move cop! Or I'll remove a couple of your vertebrae and drill a hole right through your guts,' snarled a voice quarried out of hard rock.

★

Mayor Salvo had turned off the charm this morning. With his cold dark eyes, he regarded the city's bulky director of sanitation. The man was outwardly calm, and the mayor suspected subordinates who displayed calmness when summoned to his office. Further, with a figure like that, how could he get into all those narrow corners which needed his attention? The mayor had had this critical thought before. However, they said he was the best in the nation at controlling rodent infestation, and he'd doubled his salary to lure him away from a brother mayor in an adjoining region. So he screwed down his anger. Perhaps the battle couldn't be won. He grimaced at this prospect.

He'd spent most of the night into the early hours conferring with the emergency services, being photographed at their various headquarters, at the bomb site. The town hall and his residence were thick with extra police.

But day-to-day pressures went on. Driving home in the early hours past the public library, his limousine's headlights had picked up the sinister lines of rats weaving in and out of the building. Consternation, then fury, had flared in him, his revulsion as potent as that which had overtaken him when he'd heard the bomb.

'Why is it,' he said, 'that I have to inform you that the public library has an infestation of catastrophic proportions?'

'I'm aware that the situation there is not good,' the director of sanitation said.

'Oh? Really?' the mayor sneered. His eyes bored malignantly into the other's. 'May one ask what you are doing about it?'

'Two teams are scheduled to move in next week.'

'*Next week?* Fuck! I suggest you make that today.'

The director looked doubtful.

'Well?' The mayor's eyes flickered dangerously.

'All teams are at the stadium in view of tonight's meeting.'

Mayor Salvo, frowned. 'Yes. I see. Tomorrow morning, then. *First thing.*'

'Right you are.'

'A favourable result will be expected. No excuses. I want those fucking rats *destroyed.*'

Outside the mayor's door, the director leaned his

bulky shoulders against the wall, and breathed out a long sigh. The calm exterior he adopted was his only defence against this man. The plague was running out of control. By some genetic witchery, the rats had developed immunity to the poisons. It wasn't information which the mayor would receive with equanimity, which would improve his standing with the bastard. His laboratory was working overtime – he was praying for a breakthrough.

He'd learned that his men had kept downgrading the public library's priority. They appeared to have a deep antipathy to going down into the bowels of that decayed building. He sighed ... in this city, even the rank and file pest exterminators had their hidden priorities. Tomorrow, he would kick their arses down those stairs. He wiped his brow, and went to his duty.

Following the exit of his sanitation chief, Mayor Salvo did not dismiss the contretemps at the library from his mind. Instead, he phoned a clerk in the sanitation department, who unofficially reported directly to himself, and called for a file, which duly arrived on his desk fifteen minutes later.

Though few knew it outside certain circles, Salvo was a man of honour. Quite a number had known this in the past, but most of them were dead. At one point, his clan had virtually been wiped out by rivals. His arrival at his illustrious municipal position had been via a long road of murders and heroin-dealing in the mafia's interests. He'd personally killed seventeen men, and ordered the demise of numerous others. In dispensing this largesse of violence, he'd been evenhanded between rivals, erring subordinates, politicians who'd developed independent ideas, and public officials – including a prosecuting judge and a carabinieri colonel who'd shown excessive zeal in looking into matters close to Salvo's heart. Many of his kills were pre-emptive strikes, a few were for pure pleasure.

The sanitation chief's report, on the delayed attention to the infestation in the library, had set his sixth sense vibrating. Now, as he leaned over the file, he felt a keen sense of validation. Here was something! On three occasions, paperwork showed that one particular foreman had postponed an extermination team's visit to the library's sub-basements, on what seemed like very thin pretexts.

He sat back in his deep leather chair, and mused on this. The police and the organisation's operatives had been scouring the city without success. Was the hide-out for the anarchists right under their noses? In fact, in the sub-basements of the library? Or was it a safe house for leftists or dissidents of other stripes? Might not this police inspector be found there? These propositions didn't exhaust the possibilities. Abruptly, he swivelled his chair, reached for the phone. He was put through immediately.

'My dear dottore, what do you have down in your sub-basements?' he asked the director of the public library, his charm fluently back in evidence. 'Apart from a lot of rats.' He smiled, as he listened to the brief silence at the other end.

'Why, in the basement – the stacks of dead books. In the sub-basement, the very dead books,' the director

171

reported in a puzzled tone. It appeared it wasn't a situation to which he gave much thought. But Salvo knew that between appearances and actuality could lie a no-man's territory productive of investigation.

Salvo said, 'I'm considering what reserves of municipal floorspace we've available in the city centre. Everything must earn its keep, you know, dottore. I may come back to you on this.'

When he'd put the phone down he stared across the room. Should he take a look? It might be nothing, or it might be something. If the latter, how pleasant ... and what a coup for him! With a big bang he'd go one-up on Algo. At the least, it would be an interesting distraction from the paranoia of Signora Contrera-Kant, who seemed to think she should exchange views with him each hour on the bombing. She must be driving the commissioner mad. He smiled mordantly to himself. In more ways than one!

He opened a drawer and took out an automatic, slipped it into his pocket. Then he buzzed for the head of his security detail. While waiting he linked his fingers, stretched and cracked his knuckles. He'd do a personal reconnaissance on the filthy rats, and see if he could put up some two-legged ones, as well.

*

In the grubby, basaltic building, behind the boarded-up, patched-up facade (it was going to take weeks to bring the special glass south from Milan), Leporello, the chief of security, was under pressure. He had his noon deadline very much in mind, and another customer – the local cop, Matucci – had been delivered into his care this morning, and awaited his attention. As well, he had that northern police inspector, and that crazy professor, to get hold of.

He wasn't going to waste any time on the two who'd tried to run down the De Angelis woman. In his opinion, it was not a bad idea, but strictly against the boss's orders, which left them up shit-creek. For hours they'd been stonewalling his deputy. Maybe they expected a rescue. He entered a room. The four men in the room looked up quickly, knowing instantly that things were about to change.

Leporello took a chair and calmly regarded the two large, naked, handcuffed men sitting on the other side of the wooden table. Each had dropped his gaze to the tabletop. They'd taken some rough handling. His deputy, Bartocci, and a baldheaded man with the build of a weightlifter, leaned against a wall.

'No more delays,' he said evenly. 'I want the name of your traitorous patron. Now.'

The prisoner with the cadaverous face looked up. His muscled body was as milk-white as his face. The only slack flesh was around his midriff.

'Where does that leave us?' he asked truculently out of a cut and bruised face.

'It leaves you keeping your balls,' the chief of security said concisely. 'Not a bad bargain, eh?'

'The doc and his team are standing by,' Bartocci growled. 'Four neat slits on that impressive genitalia is all it takes. Your sex life'll be a pleasant memory.'

The chief of security stared implacably at the two men with his hard brown eyes. 'Fuck the doc. Fuck neat slits. We'll do it on this table. Without anaesthetic. Chiodini will. He's from the mountains, and he specialises in doing it with sheep. Uses his teeth. Don't you, Antonio.'

The baldheaded giant, the terrorist of mountain sheep, grinned.

The cadaverous-faced man glanced at his companion. Beads of moisture had pricked out on the other's oiled, fleshy face. It streamed down the muscles and folds of his hirsute body, like mountain streams coming down overgrown hillsides.

One asked a question about their future.

Leporello gave a lying answer.

They looked unbelieving, but had no choice. The way they saw it. 'Okay,' they muttered in unison. 'We're in your hands,' the oiled-face man said. Tears had begun to run down his face.

The chief of security smiled.

Then they told him the name.

He rose to his feet and went outside with his deputy. 'Tell Chiodini to keep quiet about this. The boss wants to spring a big surprise tonight. Have those two taken out of town,' he said laconically, 'cut 'em, and kill 'em. Send the offcuts to their families, but not until tomorrow. And you stick around here.'

★

To Matucci, it seemed much longer than yesterday afternoon since he'd stood in the ruined street outside the windows of the room to which they took him. A much greater than usual sewer-stench hung in the air, had even permeated the building.

Of course a lot had happened, including his killing of the two mafia thugs, but they didn't appear to have connected him with that. It was his foray into the criminal black market for Anders' explosives which had their attention. If he came through this he'd be calling on the man who'd supplied them.

He sat in a room in his shirtsleeves. His shirt, if not quite in its early-morning mint condition, still held its creases. There'd been a body search on arrival and naturally they'd taken his pistol. He knew that the game hadn't started yet. Leporello appeared to be extremely busy, he'd darted in, fired a few questions, then rushed off again. But he'd be back – and Matucci expected him soon. He looked at his watch: 10.45 a.m. The mafia bosses would begin their meeting at the football stadium at 6 p.m, and he held close his idea of Anders' awesome, amazing plan.

Without warning, Leporello, and a man built like a weightlifter whom Matucci didn't know, entered the room. The chief of security had a film of perspiration on his brow: today was a big day. He was a man who had honed brutality to an art form, but with this cop he'd had his instructions: the commissioner's nerves were becoming fragile, he should be spared undue stress if possible. He hoped it wouldn't be possible, but he had to take care; Algo had a way of finding things out.

'Eh! Leporello,' Matucci said boisterously, 'what's this all about?' At discreet meetings he'd met the mafioso several times in company with the commissioner.

Leporello said nothing, carefully sat down on a hard-back chair, stared at the floor, as though trying to remember what he'd had for dinner last night. Chiodini leaned bulkily against the wall, and began to pick his teeth. Leporello looked up, examined Matucci's gold watch, wedding ring, glasses. 'Listen, golden boy, it's about what you were up to last night. It seems high explosive is having a revival in our city. Why would a mother-fucker, even as stupid as you, run around all night buying plastic and the makings? You tell us — and fast.'

They'd left Matucci his cigarettes. He lit up, and regarded the chief of security thoughtfully. 'It's a long story, and I don't know if you'll believe me — '

'Try me. And cut the crap, Matucci, or I'll send Chiodini here out for a blowtorch right away.'

Leporello was forty, had a hairpiece parted sharply on the right, an unblemished, olive-complexioned face shaved to perfection, and no nervous mannerisms. He was a sharp dresser, if not quite in the detective's class. Matucci observed only one contrary note: when the security boss showed them, his teeth were smeared with a brownish stain. 'Okay,' he said. 'But I'm telling you, you won't believe it.'

'Shit!' Leporello snarled.

'A detective's pay is lousy; even a chief inspector's is not so good. I have to admit it, I've got this taste for the finer things of life. But the bastards only want to demote me, the future doesn't look that bright. Yours truly is the headquarter's shit-kicker. So I figured I'd do a bit of moonlighting.'

176

He grinned confidingly. 'In my line of work you pick up on where the fat safes are, and with a few bang-bangs I figured I could get hold of a stake of folding money. Most safeblowers have a good run for the first half-dozen jobs, then they get greedy and we grab them. If I pick the right safes I won't need to strain the odds. Get it?'

Leporello stared at the detective incredulously, and Chiodini grinned his admiration. Leporello's eyes turned iron-hard. 'You crazy bastard. You think I'd believe that load of crap?'

Matucci shrugged his big shoulders. 'It's the truth.'

'So where's the plastic now?'

'In a safe place, waiting on my new career.'

Leporello shook his head. 'Jesus! What a nut case.' His eyes flicked over the detective now like a snake's tongue. 'We're showing you consideration Matucci because of the commissioner. No other reason.'

Matucci shrugged again, said nothing.

'But when I whisper some information into his ear ... ' Leporello leered showing his brownish teeth. 'Everyone in town knows you're fucking his wife — except him!' He shook his head again. 'Unbelievable! Even from you, Matucci ... '

Chiodini's admiring smile had widened.

'So when I tell him, I think we can safely conclude you'll be rat bait.'

Matucci knew the tempo was about to change. Under direct fire he might discover something new about himself. Outside a french window facing onto the courtyard, which had survived the blast, on a tiny, black-railed balcony, was a pot of russet-coloured chrysanthemums. Matucci smiled to himself. It seemed there was a flower-lover among this lot.

'You smile?' Leporello said sourly. 'How low can a man fall? You might not think so, but there's always lower.'

Matucci nodded slowly, as though this was as astute an observation as he'd heard that day. 'Eh! Eh! Leporello, I can see this might be a valuable learning experience.'

'Shut up. Last chance, Matucci. What's the plastic for? And where's the Rome cop?'

Matucci shrugged mournfully. 'I've told you about the first, about the second I don't have a clue.'

Leporello stared at the detective, then glanced at his watch. His olive complexion had taken on a tincture of red. His eyes had narrowed to slits. 'Well, I'm going to make that phone call, then we'll get down to business. You'll soon be singing a different tune.'

He got up, whispered in Chiodini's ear, then went out. Matucci took a long draw on his cigarette.

★

Anders hadn't moved for an hour. His eyes were closed. He appeared lost in deep meditation. But insidiously it had come, and he had it now: knew how it might be done. He looked at his watch – five minutes to midday; the doorbell rang. It was the courier.

Matucci had come through! Anders had everything to hand. Mark I, his spare leg, was placed on the kitchen table together with the eight kilos of plastic explosive, the two miniature time clocks, the detonators, the terminals, coil of wiring. It was years since he'd done work of this nature, since he'd attended courses designed to educate him in these matters, to protect his masters, himself, from the bomb-addicted Red Brigades. But the training had been thorough.

With a screwdriver from his maintenance kit, he opened the side of the artificial leg, and into the thigh-space, between the suction-socket and the knee, packed a good third of the explosive, kneading it into the shape of the cavity. In the centre of the plastic, he left space for the tiny clock wired to the battery terminals, the detonator.

Hand under his chin, he deliberated over the time to be set. Finally, he selected 6.20 p.m. When this was done, he stood for a long moment, inspecting his handiwork. Satisfied, he screwed the side panel back into place.

Gently he took Mark I, placed it on a chair, removed his trousers, removed Mark II, and seated, fitted Mark I, with its new heaviness, to his body. Then he took Mark II to the table.

Later, he packed his clothes and Mark II into his suitcase. Then he stood in the kitchen, drinking a glass of grappa, preparing himself, mentally, physically, for the work ahead. Carla had known that he wished to be alone this morning, presumably to work on the report, and she'd driven out of town to meet a contact. However, the only writing he was to do was to his colleague and friend, Colonel Arduini, in Rome, and he now sat down to this.

At 3.00 p.m. he closed the door of the apartment behind him. His leg was heavy and he moved awkwardly, stiffly. It reminded him of his first days with it. To be expected. The lightweight, wood-covered artificial leg had nearly doubled in weight. Most of its intricate workings were in the calf-section, but the action of the single control cable in the upper part was sufficiently impeded to give him a stiffened motion, a pronounced limp. He regretted that Carla would find the apartment empty, the typewriter unused, when she returned, would naturally have the thoughts that she would have. Then he set his mind, rigorously, to the task in hand.

Steely light strained through the pebbled glass door from the street into the foyer. When he opened it he stepped into a stark, misty afternoon; the effect was a physical shock. After fifteen hours in the draped, close atmosphere, he seemed back in the world. It gave him no pleasure.

He scrutinised the street from the doorway. All clear. Maybe. He walked in the direction of the river, found a pillarbox, posted his letter. It was addressed to his colleague's home address, did not quote his rank; it was concerned with matters relating to the regional police, did not mention his plan. Also, in a rubbish bin, he dumped a plastic bag containing the explosive wrappings and leftover wiring.

He hailed a cruising taxi and directed it to the central station. He loathed playing games, and this was a game: he put on dark glasses, pulled his coat collar up, his hat brim down, and settled back to endure for the last time the pestilent atmosphere of a taxi of this city. He smiled grimly to himself. The surly taxidriver was as usual absorbed in his own mean existence. He'd have to be careful getting out, or he might usher him from it.

'Steady,' he said to himself as he alighted, 'don't fall, don't even stumble.'

With the cafe where they'd blown up Fabri and his bodyguards behind him, he headed towards the station's entrance. As usual, the stench of carbon monoxide ruined the grace and dignity of the piazza.

'*And so we curse and strain/Towards that arcadian aperture/Beyond which lies mind's freedom.*' His ancestor-poet's destiny was to be a lost voice. A dusty, perpetual obscurity. The remembered lines, the thought, grazed his mind, then he walked laboriously under the portal into the monolithic echoing cavern, perspiration soaking his armpits.

They came at him from left and right, nearly lifting him from the ground as they turned him, pistol thrust hard into his ribs, and re-entered the grey afternoon. In the spaciousness of the big car they removed his gun, and, wordless, crushed him between their bulk in the rear seat. The air was rank with the odour of garlic, of bodies which had spent a long time watching from parked cars. His suitcase rested between his knees and the back of the front seat.

What would they think, taking him in the end as easily as this? Not these men, the men at the top. He trusted that they would not take the trouble to think about it at all.

X

THURSDAY AFTERNOON

THEY SPRINTED ALONG main streets. Anders had now stepped behind a curtain into another world: shielded by the heavily-tinted glass, he had a voyeur's view of the city's life. When the vehicle, of a kind well-recognised by many, slowed down at intersections, citizens drew back, averted eyes, as though fearful.

The mobile phone rang. The man in the front passenger seat listened, tersely responded, muttered to the driver; the car braked brutally, slithered around, headed in a new direction. Good! Anders breathed.

From now on the fate of his plan, the fruit of his great decision, depended on the validation of certain assumptions, on timing, on his nerve and steadiness – and on luck. A chancy ragbag of elements. He shouldered away extraneous thoughts, settled his mind into a quietude. He'd been taken, assumption number one was in the bag.

One of the thugs farted noisily; his colleagues gave longsuffering groans. Anders ignored them, as they did him. Their interest appeared to have shifted away from him, like fishermen when a fish has been landed.

183

★

The commissioner's hand shook as he lit a cigarette. The pulse under his eye had quickened. The pain in his stomach was feeding away voraciously. He'd spent the morning dealing with calls from his counterparts in other regions, chiefs of federal agencies.

His call for a massive dragnet across the nation had met with universal resistance; his callers couldn't square it with the degree of threat they perceived – let alone their strained budgets. According to their intelligence assessments, the bomb represented a dying gasp, not a resurgence. His region, they said – he should deal with it. He'd discovered that he had no friends; he wasn't surprised.

The worst of it was that he doubted if it *was* an anarchist bomb. He felt the insidious presence of other forces. Events were streaming past him like a secretive river in the night. Who, or what they were, were questions he contemplated with a chilled brain.

For instance, his buffoon of an ex-brother-in-law; this crazy, one-legged cop from Rome. However, the men to whom he was beholden had issued their instructions …

But that wasn't the worst of it. His whole life – his past – seemed about to implode. All of it had been gnawing away at his guts, and now a crisis point had been reached. He looked down at his shaking hands, then asked himself: 'Why can't you consider the situation calmly? In essence, is anything different from the past?'

'No, but I've reached some limit.'

They'd got his damned ex-brother-in-law. Was that the final straw? They'd plucked him from under his authority with the utmost contempt. He'd no soft feelings for Matucci. Not quite right, he had to admit. Matucci'd done his duty by Maria – much more. In a world where one's misdeeds had accumulated bewilderingly, it was comforting, at least, to have a few 'right' actions to input into the computer. In his view, looking after Matucci had been one such. Nonetheless, the man was a fool in the world in which they all had to survive. And what the fuck had he been up to anyway?

Or was it his wife's contempt – which had refined of late to a kind of toxin in his brain. Or, was it the instruction that he'd issued to arrest the octogenarian Roditi? ... The day-to-day pressures? The mayor on his back each and every day about this or that. With hatred, he considered that man of darkness. His long-running feud with Colonel Valenti of the carabinieri? With slightly less hatred he considered the colonel. The weak bastard could be relied on to take the opposing side on any question which came up, waffling on, and duck-shoving.

As for bloody Anna. He raised his eyes to the ceiling in despair at the thought of his mistress – Signora Mail Order.

None of these things in isolation – all of them in the aggregate – and, much more that had gone before. And – his notion of those massive all-knowing computers up there recording it all.

I'm going a little crazy, he thought. Delete 'a little'. Eh! Be yourself. Sit quietly at this desk, take some pills, and let it all go past. It should again become bearable.

He stared at his panelled wall, at his flickering computer screens. Several red lights were blinking angrily on the phone. The ulcer pain had settled down into a dull ache. Today he'd shit blood.

Squarely in his mind's eye came the seedy, basaltic stone building – its walls merely slightly distressed by yesterday's bomb – still guarding its secrets. Its killers. The eye roamed further, into the building's heart, to where Matucci sat in a room.

The commissioner was a smart man, knew that others thought so. And he'd always looked ahead, reflected on contingencies. He'd handpicked the two hundred strong *squadra mobile*, had lavished funds and patronage on them, had made personal friends of its leaders. If he pushed that button, would there be ignition? And *if* he pushed it? Would it be fair to all the passengers on his wagon? Did his wife really understand how tenuous was her hold on the life she led?

Perhaps she did; that would be a wonder. His two sons, at their exclusive schools, certainly could not. The *squadra mobile* might understand, but their families ... ?

He thought: fairness! He smiled an ugly smile, as he turned the notion over in his mind, like a diamond being fingered on black velvet.

He looked to the window. The light was fading rapidly. The cloud base had decapitated the taller buildings downtown. A faint reddish glow pinpointed where the sun – unseen all day – was going down. It was a long time since he'd taken the time to look across the roof tops, to watch a day finish.

The red lights on the phone seemed to be blinking faster; going crazy; any moment the knocking on the door would come.

★

The ugly, concrete-grey mass of the football stadium soared above the industrial flatlands on the city's outskirts, resembling a complex of grain silos. Looking at it through the car window Anders thought: *'an uncompromising statement.'* He recalled the hype put out by the architect, and the developer who'd corruptly siphoned off scores of millions of public money on the project in the twenties, from Roditi's first book. In its gigantean shadow, the limousine crawled circuitously towards a particular gate.

It was four. Squashed between the hotblooded bodies of his abductors, grimly, with a slowburning excitement, he ticked off assumption number two.

★

Matucci had smoked half a pack of cigarettes before Leporello returned. The bastard appeared to be rushing around like a fireman. Was so much happening? Chiodini had watched over him, reading the sports pages, occasionally cursing some player or official, responding to situations unknown to Matucci with a malignant laugh.

Leporello had three new men with him. He hadn't got through to the commissioner. There seemed to be some kind of problem at police headquarters. Time was running out, so he'd taken an executive decision. He'd start things moving with Matucci, turn up the heat, and sweat on the commissioner returning his calls.

Matucci stubbed out his cigarette. This looked like business. They studied him, then the three newcomers rushed to lay hands on him. Matucci sprang up. He kicked the nearest in the knee, and he buckled, cursing. The next instant the second had got him around the neck from behind in a headlock. Matucci was big and strong, kept fit, and had been on the streets all his life. He let his body sag, breaking the effectiveness of the grip, lowered his hips, brought his right arm back around the man's neck and hurled him up and over and across the room to crash on his back.

Chiodini, grinning, was watching this. Leporello stood aside, that same tincture of red on his face. The third newcomer suddenly had a knife in his hand.

'Fuck you, no knives,' Leporello screamed. But too late. It came thrusting at Matucci's gut, he managed to deflect it with a sweep of his hand but it slashed his thigh with a stinging pain and he cursed.

'I'll have *your* balls,' Leporello was shouting at his man. Moving fast, Chiodini deigned to take a hand. Joining the first two who'd got to their feet, he seized Matucci in a bearhug, and they had him.

'Next door,' Leporello grated. They dragged him through a doorway. Blood was streaming down his thigh, soaking through his trousers. They flung him onto a table. The room was some kind of surgery. Grunting and cursing they held him down and ripped off his trousers and underpants.

Leporello was shouting. 'Are you going to talk now Matucci? Make up your mind – fast. This is the room where we take balls off. Sometimes the doc does it. That's not for you. Chiodini will do it. He's from the sheep country and he loves biting out sheep's nuts. But he prefers cops. You won't be the same without them. If you're not a man, what are you?' He was waving his arms about.

They were holding his legs apart. Chiodini was leering in anticipation. 'I've got tomato ketchup in the cupboard. They taste real good with that,' he snarled peering hard into the detective's face.

Matucci was still fighting, and they were having trouble holding him. He was bleeding freely, but it wasn't the big artery.

'*Last chance, Matucci!* You know what we want. I've spoken to the commissioner. He doesn't love you any more. He says we're to package your balls with a little note. Send 'em to his wife. Something like: "Matucci doesn't need these any more, wants you to have them." '

He articulated the lie with relish. He was spitting out saliva as he shouted. 'Can't you see 'em at breakfast when it arrives, the commissioner saying: "What is this, my darling?" '

'Go fuck yourself,' Matucci swore, hurling his body from side to side on the table. It didn't matter now what he told these bastards. It'd only delay the issue. They'd do what they were going to do.

Leporello swore brutally. He'd gone about as far as he could go. The shadow of Algo's wrath loomed in his mind. If he turned Chiodini loose with his gnawing teeth they'd get results. But there wasn't much chance of anyone surviving that. Once the mountain man got going he was hard to stop. The phone was ringing … thank Christ!

Leporello answered, but it wasn't the commissioner. The security chief took a deep breath, became deferential. 'Yes, yes, boss. Uhuh. That's great! Understood. We're on our way!'

He wheeled around and came back to the grunting, struggling group around the table. He was grinning widely.

'Eh, Matucci! We've got Anders! And the answer on the plastic! You *stupid* prick! We've got to leave you now, but we'll be back later to tidy you up. About dinner time. Chiodini'll be hungry. Look forward to it.'

He was slapping his pockets. Not a hair of his hairpiece had been disarranged. But he hadn't been a player, just excited, just the conductor of the brutal quartet. 'Quieten the bastard down,' he snarled.

Matucci just glimpsed the blackjack coming, like a snake striking.

★

Fog rolled lasciviously across the flat country, lewdly thrust fingers into the street-end declivities of the last suburb. A misty rain began to fall, finishing the day.

Comfortable in the cushions of his rear seat, Algo smiled in the gloom as the limousine sped towards the stadium. He'd just put down the phone to Leporello.

Earlier, he'd listened to the report on how they'd

taken the northern cop, how he'd been walking with great difficulty. Taken far too easily in the light of his previous skilful evasions. Walking with difficulty. He'd known of tonight's assembly – all the police services did. A fertile mind might have assumed an appearance before it.

Algo had brought his own subtle mind to bear on it. A mind used to sorting out the most devious schemes and ambitions that men could conceive. And he'd come up with the correct answer.

A human bomb! Quite astonishing! He was certain they'd prove him right within the next ten minutes. That's where Matucci's explosives had gone! Events had moved fast in the past hour. Usually, it was the way things went. He brooded on in the murky dusk. Where do men like this come from? What stokes up their fires of desperation, when they can exist comfortably and pragmatically within the system? It was possible to understand where the anarchists were coming from, but a life-servant of a police service ... ? Perhaps the rewards, or the fear, were no longer measured out correctly.

The bomb assembled in an artificial leg – remarkable! How fortunate his interest had been stirred by the nuances in the dossier. Had this inspector really come here with this objective – or had some random factor thrown him onto this amazing path? Was he acting alone, or under sponsorship? What a superb spectacle it would make to gain the attention of the elite.

'And yesterday's outrage – was that a part of this inspector's machinations? The session ahead would be fascinating indeed. His mind rotated like a radar-dish, scanning the possibilities. He'd locked onto the northern policeman's thought processes. A ripple of irritation came: were their own clandestine patterns so discernible?

He had the name of a man locked in his mind; the man behind the Fabri killing, behind yesterday's aberration with the De Angelis woman. Leporello had reached into the minds of the two renegade toughs and extracted it like a tumour.

Ahead the road curved. A dozen or so long cars, at precise intervals, like a military convoy, rolled smoothly around the arc. Each gleamed in the following car's headlights.

★

A third man entered the room where Anders waited with his abductors. The newcomer had an air of caution, of new information. He stared calculatingly at the northern policeman. A killer, like the others, thought Anders. You could almost hear the blood squelching in their shoes.

'Come out,' he said tersely to his colleagues. Looking surprised, they hauled themselves up, and walked to the door. 'Take that off,' he said to Anders, pointing to the left leg.

When they'd taken it away, Anders sat contemplating the opposite wall. Matucci's luck must have run out. It was the only source from which they could've got that information, though maybe someone's brain had worked. He tightened his lips. He was flying on one wing now. These men were cunning in their way, but unchallenged power had bred arrogance, overconfidence, and carelessness. Or so he hoped. Anders was banking on it. Let him not run into a subtle, a more competent mind – which could think his plan through – to the bitter end.

★

Despair pierced her heart like a splinter of ice. Carla gazed at the empty typewriter, at the unused paper on the dining room table. *What had gone wrong?* The question came into her mind as a distinct voice. It was as though she'd woken from a dream, hearing someone clearly call her name. Her husband? But silence flowed through the rooms of the safe house.

Had it just been her body that he wanted?

Yet, she felt strongly that nothing had gone wrong. But where was he? She walked quickly through the flat, her heels striking into the silence, her thoughts striking similarly. If nothing was wrong, something had changed. Otherwise, he'd be here working on the report; applying his seriousness. She lit a cigarette on the move, waving the match out in the air.

Back in the dining room, she stood with her arms crossed on her breast, staring at the typewriter. His suitcase was gone. Still nothing wrong?

Near the table, on the floor, something red glinted. She went forward and picked up some tubular fragments. Some kind of flex. Wiring – sharply clipped. She stared at them in the palm of her hand. What was this?

She hesitated at the phone, eyeing it as though it were

a bomb. She took up the receiver, flicked her hair back from her face, and dialled.

'I was hoping you'd call,' the male voice said.

'What has happened?'

'He's been taken.'

Mother of God! Her hand flew to her heart.

The man coughed briefly. 'He left at 3.00 p.m., went to central station. Walked in ... it seemed like suicide. Walked in a strange way, even for him. He came out again in their clutches. They cruised back to central, then suddenly took off, went out to the Football Stadium. They took Matucci this morning, too.'

And Matucci!

'Matucci sent a warning to the professor. The police've been instructed to pick him up. Stay out of sight, he said ... The presses've been activated. Last night the cop met Anders.'

Sweet Jesus! What is he up to? Has this man from Rome betrayed us? Her heart was pounding. Everything was accelerating. She whispered urgently into the phone. 'We must get the professor out.' She glanced at the windows. It was a breath away from full dark. 'Get the car. Pick me up. Usual place. Twenty minutes.'

She put down the phone, at a half run clattered down the corridor.

Her informant hurried to the stove and turned off the gas jet beneath the canned stew he was heating.

Back in her own apartment, Carla lit another cigarette. God! she needed one. What she really needed was a drink. But better not. She stared unseeingly at the varnished faces of two of the judge's ancestors. The muscles of her face, her throat, felt tight with her excitement. Her nervous energy drove her body this way and that. Her head was buzzing. She'd have to watch out for a migraine. Take a pill now!

She glanced at her watch: 5.25 p.m. Did they know where the professor was? How much time was there? She must go. Change my shoes ...

Her throat ached with excitement. Her ideas were changing as rapidly as the come and go of spring showers. Explosives! The Football Stadium! He'd been taken there. O, God! In her mind she took a leap of faith. This Anders had *his* hidden agenda! He was still with them. She wouldn't believe anything else. Abruptly she laughed, with a trace of hysteria. 'Ha! Anders! For all your serious hidden thoughts, I think I brought you in.' Her lips sculpted the words, shot them into the rooms. She spoke to the judge's sepia-toned face: 'Whatever the outcome it's a wonder isn't it?' Yes, whatever the outcome, the conviction was spreading in her that her world, her life, was unfolding as ordained, as it should. All day she'd felt the residue of his semen in her, and now she smelt it in the room.

★

Mayor Salvo's two-car cavalcade swept under the archway into the street, and forced its way into the evening traffic. Brakes screamed. In the shadows across the road, a white sneaker kicked a Vespa to life.

Ten minutes to the river and the public library. The chief of mayoral security sat beside the driver. Two others from the security detail were in the following car. Handpicked men. Well-built, handsome even, men with a flexible view of police work; an accommodating attitude to the mayor's foibles and frequent assignments of an irregular nature.

'Something in my water tells me this'll be interesting – and profitable. So be ready, Sergio,' Salvo said from the solitary comfort of the back seat.

They shot through the traffic like a black arrow. Behind, the Vespa bounced on cobbles, weaved, wheeled in formation with a flock of brothers, who broke-up, zipped solo and raucous up the corridors between cars. Mad things, engaged in the day's last rites. All around, brakelights flared and faded.

Another fucking infestation, the mayor thought. But he was in a good mood. They braked, swung past the writers' statues, under the arch, into the public library's deserted courtyard, rocked to a halt.

'Good evening, dottore,' Salvo said pleasantly to the director who waited at this rear entrance. 'Sorry to keep you from your dinner.' He shook hands with the official.

'At your service,' the director mumbled. What was this all about?

'I must see your basements. We're deep into our annual city plan. Taking inventory of space. Otherwise how can I sleep? I'm a hands-on mayor, dottore, and the citizens are all the better for it.'

The director nodded at the possibility, said, 'This way, please.' He was puffing already. They were moving fast, the mayor and the director together, the chief of security next, then the two other officers. The mayor's driver had stayed with the cars.

At the end of the long corridor of marble was the small ornate lift. Salvo gave it a look. 'You and me, dottore,' he said. 'What about stairs?'

'Locked, for security reasons,' the director said.

'Quite right ... Sergio, you come down next with Bandinelli,' the mayor said to the chief of security. He gestured the director into the lift. 'You take the controls, dottore.'

'Which level, please?' the director asked when the door was closed.

'The lowest, of course. Where the very dead books are. And the very alive rats. And whatever else lurks in such a subterranean hell. It's illuminating, isn't it, dottore, that the dead books gravitate to Hades, so to speak? Our beloved Dante had all of that worked out, eh!'

The director pressed the button, and tried not to look into the gleaming eyes a few inches from his own. Dante! What was this philistine playing at?

The mayor smoothly drew out his black automatic, worked the action in the shadow of the director's paunch, and brought the weapon up to an 'at ready' position by his shoulder.

The director's eyes widened. For God's sake, what was the madman up to?

Having negotiated the back alleys and the garbage cans, the bug-like car crossed the bridge and entered the riverside drive. Carla, staring steadfastly ahead, now thanked God for the dense traffic here which might help shake off surveillance if there was any. They appeared to follow her part of the time only. On her right, the river shimmered like oriental black lacquer. On her left, the side facade of the public library, no longer spotlighted, rested dark and moribund. Like all cultural aspirations in this city, she thought.

They shot under the archway, and each of their hearts plunged like a skier going down an icy slope.

'Too late! Let's go,' the young man said harshly. He spun the little car in a circle, heading back for the street. As they swept in their circuit, she was craning her head at the two official-looking limousines. Empty. Except for a driver, slumped back ...

'Wait!' she said. 'Again! Go round.'

'Shit!' – the young man grated.

They did. The recumbent figure hadn't stirred. 'Pull in,' she said urgently, 'near that Vespa.'

The lift clanked to a stop. Salvo slipped out of the door, the automatic now in both hands, pointing at a dark, whispering silence – a vast acreage, in which high shadowy masses marched away into blackness. The stink of stale air and mouldering paper enveloped them.

'Jesus,' the mayor commented quietly. 'Do you have such a facility as electric light, dottore?'

'Disconnected in this lower basement. Economy,' the director said. 'I have a torch.' He flicked it on, revealing cliff-faces of books, canyons between. It gave about as much illumination as a distant star in the cosmos.

The mayor sighed. No wonder the fucking rats had made it their own. 'Keep your voice down,' he said.

'If anyone is here, they'll have heard the lift,' the director said briefly. A moment earlier it had whirred, clanked, and ascended.

The mayor moved a few paces to peer into the black mouth of a canyon. 'What's that?' he said. At what seemed a great distance, a faint glow lit up the darkness. Even as he spoke, it died away. 'Give me the torch,' he said brusquely. The director surrendered it. His academic friends were waiting for him at a favourite restaurant.

The public library soaked up sound, especially in the stacks, where all human and non-human movement became stealthy. On the marble floors of the long corridors above, most footsteps could be heard, although battered white sneakers could whisper along quietly enough.

From somewhere far above came quick multiple sounds. Muffled, distorted. The mayor cocked his head, listening. Then he heard the lift distantly clanking. Sergio ...

The mayor was drawing on his experience accumulated in stinking, dark backstreets and stairways in his earlier days. Then, much of his work, many of his murders, had been carried out under far from favourable conditions. He was not discommoded by darkness, and his feel for labyrinthine places had always been impressive. His only hangup was rats ...

Therefore, keeping the torch on his feet, he moved steadily down the canyon towards where that glow had faded out, brushing against dead men's lifework, the director shuffling behind breathing like he'd run five thousand metres. The mayor thought: The soft bastard needs a diet. He paused at a black gap in the cliff-face, felt his way into it, proceeded down the parallel canyon. What human rats' nest was he going to uncover?

She couldn't work it out. The driver in the first limousine was very dead. Shot in the head. There was a patch of blood on it like a Jewish cap. The young man had recognised the dead man. The mayor's driver! He'd taken out a large revolver. She hadn't known he had a gun. Was this connected to the professor, or was it an unrelated episode they'd stumbled on in the city's ongoing mayhem? Every citizen had a nightmare of being dragged into court as a witness of such incidents.

Whether to go forward, or retreat? ... Forward! The professor was the key to everything – their promise of a future. They entered the building, and she walked fast, shoulders thrust forward, dark hair swinging into her eyes, searching the dim corridor ahead, rubber-soled shoes masking her usual clattering walk. The young man sidled behind, a nervous rearguard.

She was almost in a trance. The black mounds near the lift had become black suits filled out with large, dead bodies. Face down. Pools of blood lay around two of the heads, like rough halos. Halos still being worked on. She was shaking. Mother of God!

The young man looked stunned. 'The mayor's security detail!' he whispered. He dangled the revolver as though he'd forgotten he had it. They stared at each other, at the empty lift-cage.

'We *must* go down,' Carla whispered tautly. The gold glints in her eyes seemed to be flashes of nerves.

'Quiet,' the mayor said. 'We're getting close.'

To what? The director was now really alarmed, and totally mystified.

Salvo could sense a kind of space ahead. A clearing in this pestilent jungle. A few more metres ... he brought the torchlight up, stabbed it towards that sixth sense-divined space. Yes! Tables, chairs, a bed, food, drink ... deliberately he moved the beam to his right.

The small man was like a statue. Frozen, spotlighted. Mane of yellowish hair, chiselled features, the octo-genarian sat quietly behind his desk, hands folded, waiting for whatever came next.

The mayor exhaled. 'Good-evening, Professor Roditi. What a pleasure. What a *great* pleasure. Would you be so good as to switch on your lights.'

The professor, squinting up the light-beam, identified the voice. 'Immediately. My dear mayor, so unexpected. But how good of you, to drop in.'

A colony of lights clicked on and pushed back the darkness to reveal the scope of the professor's work-space.

'Well, well. My compliments. So comfortable, so organised,' Salvo smiled, his snaky eyes implacably on the writer. 'What do you think of it, dottore?'

The director's face had collapsed into slackness. His mouth was open. 'What are you doing here?' he stuttered.

The mayor grinned. 'To the point as usual, dottore. That's indeed the question.' He lowered the muzzle of the automatic. 'Some of us are going to have a lot of pleasure in putting a multitude of questions to the professor. He's such a story to tell.'

The director had reverted to a stunned silence. Was this his responsibility? All thoughts of dinner had fled his mind.

Salvo turned. From the canyon along which he and the director had felt their way towards this revelation came the faintest sound. A scuffing of rubber-soled shoes? 'Sergio?' he inquired into the darkness beyond the illumination.

'Not Sergio,' a disembodied voice said. 'Put down your gun – on the table. Carefully. Turn around, slowly. Be very careful.'

The mayor did not move. His brain was working rapidly.

'I suggest you do it.'

Over the years, the mayor had heard certain nuances in speech which behoved serious attention. He did what he was told.

He put down the black automatic, turned and faced the canyon, the shadowy form at the extremity of his vision. He spread his arms. 'What is this, my friend? I hope not a great mistake you are going to regret, eh!'

The lethal red flash seared the darkness, the bullet hit the mayor in the stomach. He shrieked and pitched forward on his knees. The crack of the explosion reverberated down canyon after canyon. A fearsome sound, magnified to unreal proportions, outclassing the suffocating properties of the stacks. Dust flew in the air. Air currents sprang up.

On his knees, Salvo clutched his guts; his face was

ugly with shock. A dum-dum bullet! He couldn't let go, or they'd spill out. O Jesus. Agony! Amid the bloody hands the diamond of his ring sparkled.

The bearded young man in the green weathercoat stepped out of the mouth of the canyon. He unzipped the coat, drew the large knife from the scabbard strapped to his chest. Carefully he approached the mayor, seized a handful of the perfectly smooth but greasy hair and jerked the head back so they were face to face. The mayor's face was twisted, his eyes screwed shut. The man said something quietly, distinctly. Then a name. The mayor's eyes popped open. Then he shrieked again, and urinated. The knife came down and cut his throat from ear to ear.

The director, who had frozen against shelves at the perimeter of the workspace, collapsed. The professor leaned forward in his chair, his face tense and staring, like a person watching an intricate demonstration of which he wished to master every detail. And the demonstration wasn't yet over.

The bearded man dragged the choking mayor, whose hands had dropped away from his abdomen, to a chair, bent the head back over the wooden seat, measured the task, and with one clean blow severed it.

The professor had got to his feet, was leaning forward on the table, propped on arms as rigid as steel.

In the background, the rats were on the move, traumatised by the second explosion in recent rat-history. The bearded man bowled the late mayor's head down a canyon to the left. It bumped and slithered out of sight into the darkness, where the rats ran and twittered. He wiped the long blade on the corpse's suit, resheathed it, turned, and melted into the black labyrinth.

Carla stared at this scene, at the professor still rigid behind his desk, eyes fixed on the body. A year ago she had insisted on seeing the remains of her husband. He'd been in many more pieces than this. She could take it. At this moment, she could. The young man was vomiting copiously on the floor despite his lack of dinner. The director, still slumped against the shelves, was moving his head from side to side, muttering incoherently.

From the distance came the ancient whirring of the lift ascending. She glanced over her shoulder.

'We must get away,' she said. 'What *is* this?'

The professor appeared to be in a dream. Suddenly he began to talk in an excited voice. 'Family business, my dear. Marvellous. Marvellous! Crime and retribution! What an honour, to see such a classic exposition. I'll immortalise her name. The mayor's secretary's wife. Eyewitness! I pray I can live to record it. I've packed six boxes. Everything vital. Let's go, my dear lady.' He was still chuckling, seemed to her to have gone a bit crazy.

★

Matucci had recovered quickly. Maybe faster than they'd anticipated. They'd left him on the table. His thigh was stinging badly. He'd taken a look, it was bandaged. A blanket had been flung over him – probably the medico. The building was as quiet as the grave. He knew where most of them were. The man watching over him had looked in a couple of times, then gone back to his girlie magazine, or whatever he idled time away with.

He'd seen the tray of scalpels. He didn't even have to get off the table to reach it. Jesus, his head was aching. He selected the largest scalpel, held it in his right hand under the blanket. Not much of a weapon, but ... he started to groan, long and piteously.

The mafioso appeared in the doorway, his broad, brown face suspicious, his eyes flicking over the recumbent detective.

'What's the problem, arsehole?'

'For Christ's sake. I'm bleeding to death.' He groaned. 'Take a look at it.'

The man came closer. An obese man, peering suspiciously, breathing heavily from blocked nasal passages, his hand on the gun in his belt.

Matucci lifted the blanket with his left hand, and in a blur of movement drove the right with the scalpel into the man's prominent abdomen, ripping the blade upwards.

The man staggered back with a vast grunt, his hands abruptly gripping the scalpel; blood spurted out, he was reeling in the room, his lips articulating soundlessly, his sinuses whistling, when the half-naked Matucci sprang from the table, struck him hard across the bridge of the nose with a karate chop. He went down with a thump which rattled all the surgical equipment.

Matucci's coat and trousers were slung over a chair. He dressed quickly, one eye on the thug inching laboriously across the shiny floor leaving a long bloodsmear. More of it was bubbling out his mouth. His eyes were squeezed half-shut, focused on the door.

It hurt Matucci like hell to move, but he gritted his teeth.

In the next room, he found his pistol.

The drab back-corridors of the old building sang with silence and a cold breeze. Holding his thigh with his left hand, the pistol with his right, out of sight in his coat pocket, Matucci walked the corridors, descended stairs, grimacing. Jesus! This wasn't funny.

The detective exited by a door into the courtyard near where he'd come in early that morning. A man sat in a glass-panelled room beside it. His mouth fell open when he saw the detective coming. He scrambled up, reaching for his gun, barged out the door.

'Where the hell do you think you're going!?'

Matucci was quicker, shot him through the heart. The explosion reverberated ear-splittingly. The ice-blue eyes swept the surrounds. Nothing had moved. The detective stepped into the street, looked both ways, and walked away. 'Grade A shot, eh Commissioner?' he said to himself. A copious quantity of blood had soaked through the fabric of his expensive trousers. 'Eh, Matucci, a day to remember – or forget. Take your pick you dumb bastard.' Then he was thinking of Anders. Wasn't the investigator from Rome *still* his assignment?

XI

THURSDAY EVENING

IN A HURRY, the two big men practically carried Anders into the auditorium, his right foot barely touching the steps as they went down a short flight to the front row. They dumped him into a seat, and the one who'd carried the suitcase dropped it negligently beside him.

'Careful,' Anders breathed. Plastic was very stable, the detonator was state of the art, but everything had its breaking point.

So here he was, delivered, bag and baggage! Assumption number three validated! About thirty men sat or moved about the room, talking, greeting one another, shaking hands. More were coming down the steps each moment. Anders scanned the faces. It reminded him of any convention he'd ever attended. A few curious looks were being cast at the special arrangements being set up by several men near the rostrum.

A bunker, Roditi had called it, and accuracy was his hallmark. It was quite small, constructed of concrete, windowless, with a low ceiling. Made to order, Anders thought, with grim satisfaction. Four rows of seats were arranged compactly on two sides of the chamber, raked as in a theatre, fitted into the room tightly. Between the facing groups, slightly lower than the lowest seats were the podium and a table with several chairs. A large aluminium bench of the type seen at meat-packing premises was being set in place. It was designed to allow drainage; four aluminium buckets were at that moment being put in position under the outlets.

Ignored, except for the watchful eyes of his two guardians, Anders took in the auditorium's features. He was breathing softly, quickly. He paused at the aluminium bench, placed it immediately, accurately, in mafia history. A surge of adrenalin increased his heartbeats.

More urgently, he continued his inspection: an electric clock on the wall showed 5.55 p.m.

The atmosphere became more complex: he was under scrutiny. Men were settling down, whispering to each other, passing a message; one by one heads swung in his direction. Then, as though a switch had been pulled, the conference air was obliterated altogether – replaced by a fractile tension that shortened the breath. Suddenly, all eyes were staring at a man who had just been escorted in and sat hunched, head down, like an exhausted athlete, in a seat a few along from Anders.

Anders knew at once where he fitted in. He must have been plucked from his slaughter-line at a moment's notice. From one of his cases, a vivid memory of the screams of the pigs, as they swung along the line to the knife, came back to him.

On the elite, a deadly silence had settled.

The bang of a door, a flurry at the top of the stairs. All heads in the auditorium jerked around. Algo made his entrance. Lightly, rapidly he came down, his overcoat draped over his shoulders, his narrow, suave head turning from side to side bestowing a nod, a smile, to a favoured few. The super-elite were in the entourage that followed, moving briskly, powerfully, importantly in a phalanx – like a trolley on its rails coming down a drop; bringing up the rear, resembling a brakeman, was the black-suited Leporello.

Anders' head turned with all the others. So, here was the fabled Algo. The architect of the honoured society in modern times.

At the top of the stairs, the doors were being noisily locked and barred. Excluding the outside world, keeping evil exclusive.

Algo went directly to the podium, shrugging off his overcoat into waiting hands. The others sat down at the table. Delicately, he tapped the microphone with a long fingernail, ran a glance over one side of the room, then, turning his head, the other. A red carnation burned on his lapel – a startling counterpoint to his pale face.

He began in a quiet voice. 'Signori, you have the agenda before you. Forget it! The matters therein will be dealt with later.'

He paused, as though testing the atmosphere. 'There are two matters only which I wish to speak of tonight. First, the health of the honoured society.' He paused again, letting their minds fall in the slot. 'A kind of rot has set in. Have you noticed? I hope most of you have. Those who have not, whoever they may be ... one hopes that yesterday's foul outrage will have woken them up.' He smiled.

The audience listened with rapt attention. The sinister nuances attached to these opening remarks slid into their brains. The bombing was very much in the forefront of their minds. The bright spotlights played on gold watches, rings. An amalgam of impressions hovered in the auditorium of tanned but overweight bodies pampered in fine restaurants, in exclusive health clubs by skilled masseuses, sucked upon by expensive mistresses … of restrained, uneasy exhalations, of nerves tuning up.

'I have observed complacency, overconfidence, inefficiency – insubordination. What a catalogue! This unfortunate state of affairs has not come overnight, it's been stalking us for years, infiltrating our will, weakening our grip. The chairman's identified it' (a lie; the chairman identified nothing as he danced in the arms of morphine in his dark ballroom) 'and, those who are responsible.'

They absorbed this, were hanging on every word.

'Drastic changes will be made. All of you should look into your hearts. Are you as strong as you once were? As effective? In most regions, revenue is down.

'My friends, in the long and honoured traditions of our fellowship, blood must flow … '

He gave them silence. For a full minute. They accepted it; forty odd sets of lungs waited it out; they recognised the job he was doing on them. The more resilient brains began to consider their positions, and, like engineers doing calculations, the strength of the speaker's own foundations – the verisimilitude of the chairman's absentee status.

6.10 p.m. Jesus Christ! – was he going to bring it off? Anders gazed at Aldo's subtly moving mouth.

Then it hit him. Shot into his brain, like an acrobat responding to an entrance cue. Why are you going along with it in a daze? So cooperatively! As you did with the archbishop. The mayor, the banker, Signora Mail Order. Wake up!

His throat ached with nerves. His mind was racing now. He knew what he would do ... if there was time.

Algo's voice was going on, and he heard it in another channel. Yes, Algo had cause to be worried. The rot was there from top to bottom, the titanic organisation creaking under its longevity, under the myriad encrustations of evil. Instance: the thugs had cursorily searched his suitcase; made no connections, thought nothing through – not been supervised. They'd had it too easy for years, no opposition, no real threats. Contemptuously, negligently, they'd delivered him bag and baggage – delivered his assumptions. Super-confident, Roditi had said. Absolute power corrupts ...

6.11 p.m. He squeezed his eyes to slits: Yes! Concentrate! Be ready!

Algo surveyed the watchful faces, testing the air, a merciless eagle riding an eerily silent air-current. 'And now my dear brothers ...' he intoned to himself.

Into the silence, he said: 'I spoke of blood. Tonight, we revive an old tradition: 22nd May, 1922! And 1931! Precious moments in our history!'

A sigh moved in his listeners, like a wind coming ashore from a lake into a pine forest.

Imperiously, he raised his left hand. A man hurried

down the steps from the shadows at the top of the stairs, carrying some objects. He went to the table and put them down carefully, one by one: the Mark II leg, the wad of explosive, the disconnected time clock, the detonator. The elite craned their necks to study these items – as did Anders.

'In our midst is an assassin. An individual who believed he could slay us all. A man, who you will have heard of. That man!'

The finger pointed, the voice from the podium dropped to a whisper, the blood-red carnation seemed to flutter, and blaze with new vibrancy. 'With skill and guts and persistence and deviousness he's penetrated to this council. He's wormed his way this close! One man, a crippled, retired man! A man who came – this close!'

Mesmerised, they stared at his thumb and forefinger, held a few centimetres apart.

He'd hissed these last statements, like stabbing skewers into meat. 'It was left to me to search out this threat, to eliminate the perpetrator.'

He went on, in a more matter-of-fact voice. 'Where was the counterforce? Where was our vigilance? Well might I ask! On that table lies the evidence of the man's determination and dedication. I bring him before you. In a few minutes, I expect to hear his story, to open up this tortuous plot.'

Anders felt the weight of their collective gaze. He plunged his face into his hands. Let them have a little satisfaction. But a chill fear was rising in him. From the podium, the voice continued. 'Also among us is the other central actor tonight. Signor Perro, a master pork butcher, a worthy successor to the famous duo, Santucci and Valesio.'

Peremptorily, he signalled to the slumped man to stand up. The big tradesman, with white hair, prominent blue eyes, hauled himself up. He stood there swaying, blinking up at the rows of faces. Anders saw that his huge, pink hands were shaking. His eyes were watering. He sat down abruptly.

'He will butcher this public hero. This bitter enemy of the honoured society. Feed his mince to our regional pigs. It will be, as it was before, an act of renewal.'

Breath had been drawn, but not exhaled. The silence was absolute. Then, in the second row, a man began to clap, slowly, powerfully, the concussion smacking back from the concrete ceiling. The man! The challenger! The insight came in a flash to Anders – with no doubt at all attached to it. Another, then another, joined in, and suddenly the auditorium reverberated with terrific applause.

At the first smacking sound of applause, Algo's glance had shot to the face of the perpetrator. A slight cold smile played on his lips, a sardonic look came into his eyes. Nearby, Leporello's eyes had also gone to the face of that individual, a bulky figure in a suit of material which shimmered like steel in the light as he pounded his hands together.

Algo raised his hand for silence. 'You lead the applause, Tommaso Bugno! Thank you, my friend. Eh! You are very much in my heart.'

Another sharp intake of communal breath – hissing throughout the bunker. Those words were a sentence of

213

death. The shock was palpable. Bugno was still clapping, but in slow-motion now, making no sound, as though he was unconscious of his action.

6.15 p.m. Anders' heart was thudding, warm perspiration trickled down his spine.

Leporello's men had appeared beside Bugno, who was seated on the aisle. Suddenly several of those sitting nearby scrambled away from their seats, leaving him alone. He gazed down at Algo in consternation, then at the big men beside him; perspiration had appeared on his brow; his eyes started out of his head, his lips were working, but no sound came forth.

They grabbed him from behind and pulled him back in the seat. He jammed his legs against the seat in front, fighting for leverage. They grunted, holding him back in their vice-like paws. Veins were corded on his forehead as he fought them, perspiration flicked off his face in a shower. Abruptly, the frame of the seat-back in front cracked and splintered, and his legs were flailing to no avail.

Algo and Leporello climbed the aisle steps, like priests going in procession to a ritual. Bugno was being held now as effectively as if in a straitjacket. His head and neck were clear of the seat-top. Leporello passed Algo the braided joined cord, the stout wooden stick, with the gravity of one proffering the sacrament. Algo came in between the two men who were pinning Bugno down and deftly slipped the noose over the vigorously jerking head.

'Go fuck yourself, Algo!' the mafia boss grated.

Algo's face was a white mask. His thin white hands

twisted the stick and the cord was cutting into Bugno's swelling throat. His eyes were bulging, his mouth open, tongue flicking like a snake's. Then his bowels and bladder evacuated. Impervious to this, like a man closing an airtight door to the nth degree, Algo grunted and forced one final turn of the stick.

The assemblage were screwed around in their seats, or had scrambled to their feet.

It was over. The contender's soul had also evacuated his body. They propped the dishevelled, stinking corpse up in the chair. It stared down at the podium. The blood-vessels in its eyes had burst, and the orbs were a misty, satanic red.

Algo studied his handiwork for a moment. 'He was very much in my heart,' he announced. His breathing slightly elevated, he returned to the podium, followed by Leporello, a gratified expression on the chief of security's face.

Algo had their total attention. 'The man was a traitor.' That was enough. Most of them would know the story. He checked his notes, as though finding his place. Then with a theatrical gesture, he turned to Anders. Almost approvingly, he stared at the northern policeman. He nodded to the two men, and they pulled Anders erect, and while one held him the other began to strip off his clothes. A second nod brought the pork butcher from his chair to the bench, a narrow satchel in his hands. From it he took a set of knives and saws and placed them, shiveringly, item by item on the aluminium bench. He began to sharpen the knives on a steel. His whole body was shaking.

Five paces away, now totally naked, Anders stared at the preparations, waiting his moment. The butcher's eyes remained riveted on his tools; then flicked a glance at Anders: the watery, blue eyes were desperate.

6.17 p.m. Anders' eyes had found it: the single door, behind the top row of seats, four metres from him, in the wall of the auditorium, bearing the stylised silhouette of a man's head.

Anders touched the man on his left. 'I must go to the lavatory. I need to shit.'

The man of muscle, in his black suit, looked nonplussed. 'What?'

Anders repeated it, more urgently.

His companion said, 'There's the shit-house.' He thumbed towards the small door. 'Will I ask the boss?'

The first man shrugged, and the other stepped across to where Leporello was watching this byplay, a look of inquiry on his face. He went to the podium, and spoke quietly to Algo.

Algo was frowning at the reading stand, reappraising the questions he would put when the man was strapped down under a poised knife. The phone on the reading stand, surprisingly, buzzed. He raised an eyebrow, glanced at the chief of security, nodded peremptorily, picked up the receiver.

Anders hopped up the short flight of stairs, ahead of the two custodians, past Bugno's grotesque corpse. A fat man in an aisle seat stared at him, began to titter. Suddenly, he erupted into a belly laugh. His jowls shook, a diamond glittered in his ear-lobe. He seemed a man whose nerves were about to fracture. All eyes were on the naked man, on the pink, obscene stump of his left leg, hopping along in this comical fashion, his balls swinging, his penis flopping. One by one others joined in, until the auditorium resounded with unrestrained, almost hysterical laughter – as it had with the applause, as though they'd never seen a sight to beat it, or were trying to erase the image of what they'd just witnessed.

Anders continued on his way. It did look obscene, was comical; it was why, in his assignations with his women, he'd always disconnected the artificial leg when seated on the bed. Then, it was just one roll of his body into bliss; no comedy.

'Yes, this is the light relief. Keep ... laughing ... you bastards,' he muttered, breathing heavily as he reached the top of the stairs.

A last glance at the clock: 6.18 p.m. Even the two sullen custodians were grinning. One opened the door, looked inside, and gestured to him to enter. He went in: a small windowless cave in the concrete wall of the auditorium: a single bowl toilet, with a wash basin. They allowed him to close the door, knowing there was no way out, more for their consideration than his.

'Fast!' one said, and turned away with his colleague to look down with interest on the meat-packer's bench, which had now been spotlit.

Quietly, smoothly, Anders slid home the bolt. He sat down on the bowl, raised his arms, gripping each elbow with a hand, bracing them in front of his face.

Here was an island of peace. Now he would just wait. This is for all of you, he thought. Every prosecuting judge, investigating magistrate, policeman, carabinieri, who's sacrificed their life. Rest in peace.

Above all, it was for Anton Anders.

Then Montaigne's words flashed into his head: 'Death is the receipt for all evils.' If it was an epitaph for him as well – so be it.

Outside the laughter had died. Algo had his questions in order. He also held in his mind the surprising news. The failure of a protégé on whom one had lavished care and attention was always a shock. The commissioner. He'd blown out his brains. The stupid, stupid man. His failure, or mine, he wondered, and put it aside for the moment.

He waited, frowning impatiently. His eyes travelled to the pork butcher, to where the northern policeman had been sitting, to the suitcase.

His heart became ice. 'What is that?' he hissed at Leporello.

The chief of security started. Hurriedly he consulted a subordinate. 'The condemned man's clothes, his spare artificial leg … '

Algo's eyes shot up to the lavatory. He screamed: *'Get it out of here!'*

Leporello drove his athlete's body out of his chair like a sprinter coming out of the blocks. Forty other bodies jerked forward as though on a string, their faces taut, inquiring …

Anders never heard the explosion, didn't register the door as it blasted in, felt nothing as it smashed him against the toilet wall like a manikin in a simulated auto collision.

XII

THE POET

TEN DAYS HAD PASSED, and autumn was on its deathbed. The trees along the streets were as naked as Anders had been in the auditorium at the Football Stadium. From the central station, Anders stared across the piazza. Like particles of ice, the glass from the investigating magistrate's bombing still glinted dully in the trunk of the plane tree.

He thought: the debris of disaster surrounds us. It had taken two days to clear up the body fragments from the auditorium: forty-odd ex-human beings in squelching, plastic bags; only two bodies – his escorts – had been more or less intact. Scrubbing the tornado of tissue, bone and blood from the walls had been quite a task. The murder squad had been surprised at the number of handmade shoes that contained feet when most of the rest had been fragmented.

He turned his back on the cafe, and awkwardly, on the crutches, moved towards the station's main entrance. He thought of the last time he'd entered it, which, though only ten days ago, seemed like it'd been in some distant era of his life.

At his side, carrying the newly acquired bag, Matucci matched his pace. He, too, was moving in a slightly constrained way.

Matucci said, 'I thought my ex-brother-in-law had more guts.'

'Very unusual,' Anders said, considering the commissioner's demise. 'An act of conscience, I believe. I fear a number'll find that way out expedient.'

'As for the mayor ... '

Anders grinned, painfully. 'It gives you faith, that the big lottery can come up with a winning ticket.'

'Eh, it does!' Matucci laughed boisterously. 'About forty of my colleagues – the top brass – are not taking kindly to their arrest and interrogation. Your Colonel Arduini and his colleagues from the capital are being merciless.'

The ice-blue eyes glittered ironically at the northern policeman. 'Where've these upright and earnest colleagues been all these years?'

Anders grunted with his effort. 'Do you know what Andre de Chenier said two hundred years ago?: *"Before the Terror worthy men retreat/Kindness dies, and virtues grow discreet."* That's the picture, my friend. Like me, they've been sitting on the fence, full of reservations, even hatred in some cases, but rusted into inaction. Those that weren't corrupted themselves. In essence: short of balls.'

Matucci shrugged, raised a hand to the high and mighty steel-structured ceiling. 'Inspector, you came through with a bang.' This time, he laughed uproariously.

They stopped in the midst of the vast concourse. The

four plain-clothed police from the ministry stood around them in a rough circle, their vigilant eyes scrutinising innocent citizens.

Anders' eyes found the flower stall; the sunflowers were gone, hothouse blooms had appeared. And, Judge De Angelis was standing there in an alcove, and they had eye-contact. He looked exactly the same as the photograph on his desk – except his sensuous lips were moving, under his clipped, black moustache, and he was shaking his head wearily, reprovingly. Mind-to-mind the words came across the concourse to Anders: 'I understand, of course, why you did it. But it's not the way.'

Anders stared; the image dissolved; he saw again the hothouse blooms. That bloody explosion. His brains were still scrambled.

Beside him, Matucci rocked on his heels, waited for him to speak. With an effort, he came back to their conversation.

'You and I know where it all stands. A little time's been bought. A breathing space. Perhaps, it can be parleyed into something more substantial.' Anders mopped his brow, the crutches were hard work. 'But the head cut off, the roots intact. What does that mean?'

Matucci was scanning the concourse.

Anders stared towards the stripe of grey light at the end of the great roof where the platforms debouched into the open. 'Some thinkers tell us that in the universe there's neither good nor evil – neither rhyme nor reason – just an echoing indifference.'

Matucci tossed the bag to one of the escorting police.

221

He grinned. 'Well, they'd seem to be on the right track, wouldn't they?'

Anders said, also smiling. 'Too true. As for the Salvos, the Rastos, the Contrera-Kants – unfortunately there are always others ready to step into their shoes. A new crop. Although, Signora Mail Order would be a hard act to follow.' The surviving members of a cabal were currently being grilled by a phalanx of investigating magistrates.

They shook hands. The detective had been reinstated to his former rank. It was hardly a reward, Anders thought. He would be absorbed in calculating the time that he had, and the best way to use it.

As for himself – now a national hero twice over – he was an icon to be tracked down and destroyed. His death, preferably in a noteworthy and public way, would be a necessary way station en route to the reassertion of mafia power and supremacy.

He smiled. 'Good luck, Matucci!'

'Take care, Inspector.'

The train went out into the grey landscape. Anders gazed at the obscurity, and remembered with intense pleasure, and great affection, the remarkable luminous qualities of Carla and Cinzia.

In Rome, a week later, on a freezing afternoon, he spent two hours at an establishment which he'd frequented now and then for years. To himself, he called it 'The Dream Palace'. He had an affectionate and enjoyable reunion with a very old friend. Her curves, and declivities, were as familiar to him as his homestead road to a farmer.

Having known Marks I and II, this friend was most interested to see, to have explained, the technological advances in his new leg.

Walking in Via del Corso that evening, giving it a test-run, he saw young men and women assistants building great stacks of red-jacketed books in the display windows of Schostal, the famous bookstore. As he watched, they lowered into place a huge photograph. The yellowish hair, the puckish, fox-like face, twirled gently on its suspending threads – emblazoned across its chest in black letters was: *Rigor Mortis II.*

He walked on, thinking that Roditi could not have had more auspicious timing for the launch. The mafia was in complete disarray. This book would reach the citizens – though he would not have time to read it himself. Every hour would be needed for his book on the poet.

A few days previously, and it was still there, Carla's beautiful face with its fighting-to-maximise-the-advantage expression had stared at him from newsstands.

With the massive complicity of the ministry, he'd avoided the press and he'd smiled at his ten-year-old photographs.

A large, sealed carton had arrived at the ministry, addressed to him. They'd put it through the X-ray machine, listened to it with a stethoscope device. Seemed to be only paperwork. Nonetheless, his colleagues had stepped outside while he opened it.

It was from Professor Roditi. A scrawled note of appreciation – and packed tightly into shoe boxes, wad after wad of faded letters in their postmarked envelopes.

Smelling faintly of herbs, each bundle tied with a black ribbon.

Anders was stunned. The remainder of the poet's letters to the love of his life – right through the late 1860s! He had to sit down. Long letters, reporting on his life and work ... His colleagues had reappeared and they opened a bottle of wine. Clearly, from this dazed public hero's demeanour, something momentous had occurred.

Holding the glass, Anders was wondering, still in a daze, that while the archives of their country were notoriously inaccessible, the professor's penetrative skills would be hard to match.

That evening he packed two bags, several cartons, and making maximum use of his evasive skills disappeared from the city. He went further north to his poet-forebear's birthplace – the place where he, Inspector Anders, late of the Ministry of the Interior, holder of two Presidential Commendations, had been happiest in his life. He took a room in a private house overlooking the verdant, tangled hills, but not itself overlooked from any point.

The next morning he sat down at a worktable, and assembled the boxes of index cards containing his research: the intensely personal detective work of thirty years.

Downstairs, the woman who he was boarding with hummed an old song to herself as she prepared *gnocchi di ricotta*, by special request. She was about sixty, with wavy, white hair, wide shoulders, solid but not unshapely legs, intelligent, reflective eyes – and breasts, that when released, would tumble down on her stomach. She had about her, an intriguing atmosphere of family problems buried in the past. But Anders had seen the smile come to her sad, oval face.

At last. The window was open. He took a long breath of the town's clean air.

He took up his pen and began to write: *'Anton Anders was born on the 20th of January, 1832, on the evening of the feast day of Saint Sebastian, in the small mountain town of ———— ... '*

He had a strong feeling that his last mission had taken him into the country of phantoms, a period of unreality, a dream-time, and that now, he was going further into similar territory. And it was strange: he no longer heard the poet's voice in his head.

The most substantial thing close to him, lying on his worktable, was the blue metal barrel and the burred stock of the 9 mm Beretta. He estimated – hoped – he might have twelve months to complete what he considered his main life's work. Not long. But, whether one acknowledged it or not, or forgot it from time to time, was not all of life a helter-skelter race to the eternal darkness?